fiona

me a river

6thin XFiction

find
me a river

BRONWYN BLAKE

Lothian
BOOKS

For Piper

Acknowledgements
My profound thanks to the following people and organisations:
Bryan Dwyer and the Bendigo Regional Institute of Technology,
Castlemaine campus. Julianne Charity, remarkable lip-reader and
friend. Jason Eades, Ramahyuck District Aboriginal Corporation,
Sale. Danielle Zanetti, Cathrine Harboe-Ree, Anna Cutler and
Agnes Nieuwenhuizen. The May Gibbs Children's Literature
Trust, Maurice Saxby National Mentorship Program.

Thomas C. Lothian Pty Ltd
11 Munro Street, Port Melbourne, Victoria 3207
www.lothian.com.au

National Library of Australia
Cataloguing-in-Publication data:

Blake, Bronwyn.
Find me a river.
ISBN 0 7344 0261 9.
I. Title.
A823.3

Cover design by Michelle Mackintosh
Cover photograph by Sonya Pletes
Text design by Paulene Meyer
Printed in Australia by Griffin Press

Chapter 1

KES BALANCED ON the narrow cliff ledge. With her back braced against the hot rockface she watched her namesake, the kestrel, sweep across the ravine. Its shadow crossed her eyes. The red rock burnt her back and her bare feet.

She leapt forward, spreading her arms, crying out the kestrel's strange call, 'ki-ki-ki', as she plunged into the waterhole five metres below. The water closed over her head and for moments the world was still, cool and silent, filled with a million streaming bubbles.

Kes floated up gently, watching the shimmering silhouette of her younger sister form against the cloudless sky. Sarah was sitting in her favourite tree, a single gum that jutted out of the cliff face high above Kes. She'd rigged up a comfortable cushioned hammock in it.

'Aren't you going back to meet them?' Sarah called as she surfaced.

'In a minute.'

'Do you want me to come? I will if I have to. I suppose.'

Kes laughed and rolled onto her stomach. She opened her eyes in the clear tannin water and watched the tiny creatures of the waterhole floor scattering from her. Kes duck-dived, following an elver as it fled for its hollow log.

She knew what it was the instant she saw it, half protruding from the black tree trunk into which the elver had disappeared. Submerged in the deepest part of the waterhole, Kes had rediscovered the carved bird she'd taken from her father four years ago.

She'd wanted it close to her because it was so precious to him. Like the gold grape brooch with the translucent green stones that had belonged to her mother's grandmother. Her aunt Mai had rescued that from one of the chook sheds.

The bird looked smaller, its pointed beak less threatening. Kes rubbed the black slime gently off its belly with a handful of sand. For a second she wondered if it was the one she'd stolen so many years ago, but the patterns were still there, barely visible after its years of immersion. She turned the carving over and traced the circular incisions on its back. She knew now that it was a brolga displaying, its wings spread. Years ago it had danced on two legs, now it'd have to make do with most of one.

She held it up against her face and could hear her father's gentle voice as if it were yesterday.

'Kes, it was an accident. You should've asked, but

you didn't mean to lose it. Those birds can't swim, not like real ones.'

She hadn't understood her mother's fury, 'It's the only thing your father has of his family. Now you get out there and find it.'

The ten-year-old Kes had protested, 'But we're his family, us four kids, and you, too, Mum. With the Lawsons as well, he's got nine of us. We're his family.'

She remembered the incident so clearly. As she was howling and running for the door, her father had grabbed her and continued gently, 'Now why would I need a wooden bird when I've caught a real live kestrel?'

Over the years Kes had searched the billabong for it, and now, chasing eels, she'd finally found it.

'What is it? What did you find?' One of her brothers leapt off the rock wall and bombed into the water beside her.

'Don't, Jon, you idiot. You nearly landed on me.' Kes trod water, 'It's a carved bird I took from Dad years ago. You wouldn't remember it; you and Jack were only six. I got heaps from Mum. She was so mad! Said I wouldn't get another meal until I found it. I never did … find it, that is.'

She waved it at her sister up in her reading tree on the cliff face. 'Sarah! Remember this?'

'Couldn't forget it if I tried! You dragged me in here, bawling your head off, made me look for that ugly thing until I was nearly drowning, with Mum pacing up and down the edge swearing at you.'

Kes laughed. 'That was the first time I ever heard Mum swear in front of us kids. I gotta go and check out this Brian kid. I hope he's all right 'cos we've got him for the whole weekend. Angie says he's OK, but that doesn't mean a lot, she's such a softie.'

The old truck never started when it had been sitting in the sun. Kes jumped out and shouted to her brothers, 'You'll have to push it.'

They came reluctantly out of the waterhole, shoving each other, dripping and complaining. Kes climbed back into the cabin. The steering wheel was too hot to handle and the cracked vinyl seat burnt and pinched the back of her legs.

'OK. Go!' The back wheels were stuck in last winter's tyre rut, hard as concrete.

Sarah hung her book over a branch. 'You want me, too?' she called to her brothers.

'No, you're useless.'

Sarah smiled. She swung down onto a lower branch of the tree and dropped the last few metres into the water. By the time she had swum across the billabong, the truck was rolling slowly down the track. A couple of shuddering jolts and it started.

'Thanks,' Kes yelled back. 'Take care, you three. Don't drown each other before I get back.'

One of these days, Kes thought, driving slowly up to the houses, her old Ford would finally die, shaken apart by this mangling track. No, it wouldn't. Finn Lawson, 'cousin-without-imperfection', could fix anything. He'd just re-floored it with the flattened kero tins that were now burning the soles off her feet, and mended everything else in it with fencing wire, door springs and ingenuity.

Kes told her cousin that the truck was 'a canvas on which you can display your mechanical genius' and that 'genius dies without constant practice.' Finn wasn't convinced.

The herefords in the home paddock heard the truck and came charging up from the she-oaks in the dried-up creek bed. They hoped the truck meant hand-feeding.

Kes watched them trailing the truck in the rear-vision mirror. A year ago they had been prime breeding stock, but now they looked like bony scrubbers, and summer was still officially a month away.

Halfway between the waterhole and the houses, Kes crossed the cattle grid, leaving the beasts milling around the fence behind her, bellowing with frustration. They'd lost a lot more condition even in the past few days. Some of the weaker ones were having trouble keeping up with the truck. Poor scraggy beasts, the drought had made grass so hard to scavenge, they lived in constant hope of a hand-feed.

She stroked the bird on the seat beside her. Pat, her father, would be delighted. He was such a quiet man, unlike the rest of the family who were so loud and forceful that Kes sometimes wondered how he'd ever ended up with such kids. Finn, who thought before he opened his mouth and yelled, was more like him than any of his own four.

The track followed the fence, lined with dusty eucalypts, up a long gentle slope to the two farm-houses; her family's house, and its twin on the far side of the orchard, belonging to her aunt and uncle and their two kids, Finn and Angie Lawson.

The position of the houses on the crest of the gently rounded hill at the highest point of Federation Plateau, gave them an uninterrupted view deep into the Baw Baw ranges; sequential folds of deepening blue horizons, fourteen of them. Kes counted them every morning from her bed. Iridescent grey by first light, golden at sunrise, green in spring, occasionally white in winter. Kes glanced over at them and sighed. Now they just looked tired, half hidden in heat haze and parched brown by the drought.

About a kilometre away from the house yard, she took a side track to bring her around past the chook sheds. She needed to check the birds' water supply; this weather was far too hot for them. Yesterday, three more layers had died.

A rabbit skittered out from the shade of the gums, racing blindly across the track and Kes swerved to avoid it. Even though they poisoned rabbits regularly and ripped their warrens, she could never bring herself to run them down. The dust puffed up around the truck's wheels and drifted away into the paddocks.

Kes slowed to a crawl as she came along the front of the row of chook sheds. Chooks, thousands of them, were the secondary business of the farm. She leaned out the window to check on their troughs. In this temperature, if the automatic drip feeders clogged, the watering system could dry up quickly and then the chooks keeled over from heat exhaustion.

She drove across the house yard, passing the verandas of her own century-old, white weatherboard house, built by her great-grandfather to replace the original slab hut. She went through the orchard and past the vegie garden, past the old Victorian bird aviary with its ornate green and gold lacework, and parked under the Lawsons' sitting room window. Her younger cousin, Angie, was hanging out the window, watching to see if she'd brought Sarah.

Angie and Sarah, Sarah and Angie; they were like two circling twin stars, never far from each other's path. It was easy, at first meeting, to think of Sarah, the louder and more vigorous, as the natural leader, but like orbiting bodies it was impossible to say who led and who followed.

Kes stood up on the running board of the truck so she could talk to Angie across the cabin roof. 'What's the matter? Are they awful?' she whispered, grinning up at her cousin.

Angie made a face at Kes and stuck her fingers

down her throat. It didn't look to Kes as if the visit of Brian Conroy and his parents was a raging success. They'd now been there over an hour.

'How much longer?' asked Kes.

Angie shrugged, then abruptly disappeared inside the room.

Kate Martin, carrying buckets of eggs to the stone coolstore under the Lawsons' house, paused beside her daughter.

'Angie's just been caught hanging out the window being uncomplimentary about the visitors,' Kes said. 'Hey, Mum! Guess what I found? You can start feeding me again.'

'What?'

'You know, "You'll never get another meal until you find that bird, Kes Martin!"'

'You didn't! Oh, Kes! That's wonderful. Is it — OK?'

Kes reached into the truck. 'A bit battered and stained by the mud and tannin. I was chasing an eel and I saw it half buried in an old hollow log. It's lost a leg and a bit, but it's not too bad considering it's been in the waterhole for four years.'

Kate turned it over, smiling. 'I'm so glad. Pat'll be thrilled. You know it's the only connection he has to his family.'

'Yes, Mum. Loud and clear. Like it was yester-day. I also remember language unbecoming to a parent. Language I hope never to hear again from my mother's lips. I've gotta meet the Conroys, I'm late, the truck didn't want to start — well, actually I didn't want to get out of the water. What are they like?'

'I don't know, I only said hello as they arrived.' Kate smiled. 'But they didn't look too prepossessing ... they're very ... fashionable ... you know, trendy-looking. Here, take these eggs to the coolstore, will you, please? I need to get the tomatoes as well.' She cut through the orchard, calling back, 'And I'm really glad you found the brolga, Kes.'

Chapter 2

DOUBLE GLASS DOORS opened up the Lawsons' living room to wide verandas overgrown with spreading grapevines. The cattle dogs lay in the shade, panting. The pup, standing on her mother, was trying to eat the grapes. Beyond the verandas, the cleared house block, the home paddocks with great stands of shading trees, and then the forested foothills stretched away into the Baw Baw Mountains.

Kes jumped up onto the veranda. The dogs were so hot they barely lifted their heads, except the baby, Ella, who leapt for Kes' feet. The girl stumbled over the puppy and stopped awkwardly in the doorway. The Conroys looked at her as if she'd escaped from captivity. They were beautifully and expensively dressed.

Damn, thought Kes, at least I should've combed my hair.

Her uncle Charlie Lawson suddenly smiled, 'Come in, Kes. Come and get a cool drink. Kids still at the waterhole? Much better down there in this heat, isn't it?'

'Yeah. I suppose so. I mean — yes. It's a bit cooler down there.'

'Airconditioning would be such a help in this room,' said Mrs Conroy.

Kes leant against the doorjamb wondering if she still had time to escape and clean herself up. She was acutely aware of the dust from her clothes rising in puffs every time she moved, drifting through the shafts of sunlight and wafting around the room.

Her aunt smiled at her and indicated a seat, 'Come and join us, Kes.'

'I won't sit down, Mai, I'm caked in dust. I'll sit on the doorstep.'

'This is my niece, Kes Martin,' Mai said to the Conroys. 'Kes has been down at the billabong with her younger sister and brothers. Brian might enjoy cooling off down there after his long trip.'

The Conroy parents barely acknowledged Kes' presence. Mr Conroy glanced at her and went on talking to her uncle. Mrs Conroy looked her up and down, stared at her dusty bare feet and turned back to her aunt. Brian Conroy gave a half smile in response to her greeting and went back to examining his hands. Kes shrugged and shot a quick look at Finn, hanging out of his cane chair. She thought he was going to explode — with exasperation or laughter — she couldn't tell which.

From her spot on the doorstep, she watched the sunlight pooling on the polished wooden floorboards, flickering across the walls and faces of the seven other people in the room. It looked like reflections of water — as if she could paddle her feet in it.

At the other end of the room, Angie stared angrily out the window. The lace curtains breathed in and out on gusts of hot north wind. A tendril of the old vine knocked against the window frame. A brilliant dragonfly hovered in its shadow, twitching, poised to dart away.

Brian, Finn's age, hunched in the corner of the couch opposite, was surreptitiously watching her.

Kes smiled at him, 'Hot, isn't it? It's better at the waterhole.'

He looked away. Apparently he only spoke when he was forced to. Angie turned from the window and scowled at him.

Brian's mother sat in one of the cane armchairs, slowly fanning herself with a magazine. She looked like a camouflaged animal; the skin of her face and bare arms was striped by the diagonals of the vine lattice and mottled by its green light. She reminded Kes of a reptile in waiting.

Kes's aunt, Mai Lawson, a tiny Chinese woman, sat at the table beside her, pouring endless cups of tea and answering the woman's complaints with her generous smile. How could Mai be so patient with her? Kes wondered.

Mrs Conroy kept including Angie in her conversation, making slightly barbed comments in a babyish voice that Kes found intensely irritating. Kes wondered if she really were as helpless as she pretended. She looked like a shop window dummy with false eyelashes, teased hair sprayed stiff on top of her head. But Kes bet she always got her own way.

'I do envy the young,' Mrs Conroy smiled at Angie. 'They are so relaxed now, in their dress.'

Angie looked shocked. She'd even put on shoes and a dress for the visitors. Certainly, it was just an ordinary sort of old cotton dress, the blue daisies a bit faded, but for someone who lived in bathers, shorts or jeans, it was like dressing up. And she'd brushed her hair and got it to stay down for once. She blushed with embarrassment.

Kes opened her mouth to defend Angie but Mrs Conroy turned away from her with a half smile to say something softly to Charlie beside her, who nodded and went on staring at his boots. Kes shut her mouth and wondered if she should go and sit next to Brian. He looked completely out of it.

'Do you want to go swimming, Brian?' she asked. 'The waterhole's not as big as it used to be but it's still got water in it.'

Brian shrugged and grunted a reply that could've meant yes or no. Either way it wasn't too enthusiastic. He stared out the doors past Kes.

Mai asked Finn to hand the tea to the visitors. He lifted his lanky body out of an armchair and slouched across the room. He was bored witless, and the heat wasn't helping. Finn looked as odd and uncomfortable in his good clothes as Angie. His thin legs stuck out the bottom of his cotton pants; he'd grown out of them over winter, and his short-sleeved cotton shirt stuck to his back with perspiration. With his hair plastered onto his forehead like black plastic strips, he looked like a skinny Lego man.

Finn winked at Angie as he passed. 'Charming parents!' he said, without a sound.

Angie nodded faintly. Kes hid a smile. That was the great thing about Angie being deaf — you could have a whole conversation with her without uttering a single sound.

Angie crossed the room and sat on the couch next to Brian. Kes heard her ask him something about swimming down at the waterhole, then about a kid they both knew from hospital. His replies were grunts or single words. Angie was the only one of them who knew him at all. When their stays in hospital coincided, Angie and Brian spent a lot of time together. It was hard for Kes to understand the attraction Angie felt for him, but maybe he was different away from his parents.

Angie, now twelve, had been born profoundly deaf. She had virtually no hearing, but she had learned to lip-read early, and now could speak almost as well as any other kid in the family. She was amazing. She could lip-read halfway across the yard. No one ever got away with anything if Angie could see them.

It didn't make any difference to Angie if you spoke out loud or formed the words silently, except, as she said, 'People speak clearer when they have to be silent. Especially Finn, who's usually too lazy to open his mouth and mumbles.'

Surely the Conroys would have to go soon, Kes thought. They still had a long distance to travel. She watched Brian. He was sixteen, barely a year older than Finn. A good-looking boy; he'd obviously dressed carefully in the very latest gear. Every stitch he wore was the latest brand name.

Across the room, Brian's father was speaking at a volume no one in the room could ignore. 'Shouldn't wonder if the young chap made house captain next year. Eh, Brian, isn't that right now? He's the most popular fellow in his year, aren't you, son? Teachers think the world of him, too, don't they, Brian? Tell us. Don't be shy now — amongst friends.' Kes had a fleeting moment of sympathy for him.

Brian scowled at his father, 'If you think you know, you tell them.'

Brian's father smiled at him indulgently. His mother tittered and said to Mai confidentially, 'Ooh, he gets so embarrassed when we say nice things about him.'

Who gives a stuff? thought Kes.

Angie got up from the couch, walked to the window, pulled back the curtain and hung out. Brian's mother pursed her lips at her back in disapproval.

Below her, her aunt Kate paused and looked up, amused at the sullen face in the window. She was carrying a box of windfall apples down into the cellar. 'How's it going?' Kate asked soundlessly.

Angie stuck her thumbs down.

Kate smiled, saying, 'Not much longer,' as she disappeared down the stairs. For an instant the cool smell of apples and drying herbs drifted up past the window; it was like an aromatic wash over Angie's hot face. She wondered for a brief moment what would happen if she climbed out the window and down the grapevine. She couldn't work out what had got into Brian; he was being such a pig. First she couldn't get him to speak at all, then he'd been rude to Finn, and now to Kes.

Finn flopped back into the big armchair by the veranda doors. He shut his eyes and tried to stop listening. All he wanted was to get out of the house and down to the waterhole.

Mr Conroy drew breath, waiting for Charlie Lawson to reply to his last declaration on the response of the National Party and the Federal Government to rural drought. There was a long silence. Finn smiled to himself and opened his eyes. His father had tuned out too; he was staring blankly into space. He hadn't even heard Mr Conroy.

'If you'll excuse me, I'll just go and check on the chooks,' said Kes, standing up.

'I'll help you.' Finn leapt up, suddenly awake.

His mother glared at him and asked him to hand around the cake. His father looked almost as distraught as he and Angie. Finn glanced pleadingly at both his parents, desperate to get a break from the monologue that Mr Conroy was starting again; it was more interesting listening to the drone of the blowfly circling the ceiling fan.

'Angie, offer Mr Conroy a scone, please,' said Mai.

Mrs Conroy gave Angie one of her special smiles and murmured, 'Sweet Angel.'

Angie cringed.

'Angel of deaf,' Finn said silently. Angie giggled. Mai scowled at both of them and their father Charlie rolled his eyes and shifted around impatiently in his chair.

Angie and her mother regularly made the long trip into Melbourne to the Royal Children's Hospital. During these visits, and because Angie and Brian seemed to get on so well during their hospital stays, Mai pursued the acquaintance with Mrs Conroy. She'd invited Brian only two weeks ago to come and stay for a weekend.

Brian's parents had rung without warning that morning. They were near Moe on the Princes Highway, on their way to Orbost. Driving was troubling Brian's ears and he was feeling carsick. Was it possible to take up Mai's offer at such short notice? Mai, soul of kindness, said that of course it was no trouble. He was to stay for the weekend.

So here they all sat, on the edges of their chairs. Inside! On a day like this! Charlie Lawson, like a caged cat, looking as if he was going to explode; Mai, kind and welcoming. The Conroys telling endless stories about the gifted and admired, popular and talented Brian, how they thought he might even be school captain next year.

You do have to feel sorry for him, I suppose, Finn thought. I'd kill Mum and Dad if they went on like that. If I hadn't died of shame first.

'Where do you go to school, Finn?' asked Mrs Conroy.

'Moe Secondary College.'

'What, every day?'

Finn looked at his father in despair. 'Yes, of course.'

'But that must be a hundred kilometres away. I thought we'd never get here today, so isolated! Interesting — I suppose — but so far for school! How do you get there?'

'It's only sixty-five ks. We catch the school bus. All six of us.'

'But that's much too far to travel every day! You must go to a proper school, a boarding school in Melbourne. Insist on it, Finn.'

Finn was furious: would this woman never give up? 'That'd be the last thing I'd do. I love living here, and Moe Secondary College *is* a proper school. What do you think we are? Do you think we're a pack of back-of-the-mountain hicks?'

'Finn! Don't be so rude,' said Mai.

'Sorry,' mumbled Finn.

'You don't know what you're missing,' Brian said.

'I know what I'd miss all right, my family and the bush. I'll never swap this freedom, this space, unless I'm forced, certainly not before I get to uni. Anyhow, I like going to school where I live. My mates all live around here — well, within fifty ks or so.'

'Don't always want to be relying on mates, you know,' Mr Conway said loudly. 'Boarding school's the thing for you country boys. It'd make a man out of you. Teaches young boys independence. Gets them away from their mothers' apron strings.'

'With any more independence I'd never see my kids,' said Mai. 'Anyway both of them in boarding school would be far too expensive — prohibitively so, I'm afraid.'

'Didn't mean the girl. Just the boy. Important for boys.'

Angie glared at him. Sexist pig, she thought. He looks like one, too, with his piggy red face and the hairs growing out of his nose and ears.

Mr Conway's eyes swept past and through her as

if she had no substance. Charlie Lawson smiled at his daughter's angry face and gave Finn a ghost of a wink.

Angie clenched her jaw and stared out the window. This visit was not going at all the way she'd wanted. If Brian says one more dumb thing, just one more, I'm going to take him outside and bash him up, she thought.

In the momentary silence, Finn heard the truck coming back from the chook sheds. Through the grapevines, he caught the flash of rusty red as Kes drove up to the veranda again. Good old Kes, he knew she wouldn't have deserted them. Come back to rescue them from the torments of the Brian Conroy fan club; membership two and not increasing.

Brian, his mother was saying, was a wonderful swimmer, he'd have made the school team if he'd been able to compete, but he wasn't allowed to swim. He had tubes in his ears. Tubes in his brain, thought Finn. A hose pipe.

Kes came back into the living room. Finn laughed at her and she gave him a dirty look. She hadn't been near the chooks. She'd gone over to her house, changed her clothes, put on sandals and done her hair. She'd missed a bit when she washed her face. Mrs Conroy stared at the muddy streak down her cheek.

'Come here, Kes,' said her uncle, perching her on the arm of his chair, his arm around her waist. 'Tell us how many kids you've managed to drown since breakfast. If you haven't done in either of the twins, you haven't been trying hard enough.'

Angie caught her mother in the kitchen and said, 'I don't think it's a good idea having Brian for the weekend. He's being stupid and rude to everyone.'

'It's a bit late for that when he's already here,' Mai replied. 'Anyhow, Angie, I don't see how you can say that. You don't know the boy very well, he's only just arrived, and he looks more upset than anything else.'

'I do know him, Mum. Better than you. Far better. We've spent ages together in the hospital … weeks and weeks. You get to know someone really well in hospital. He's being stupid and I don't know why.'

'Enough about stupidity, Angie, calling others stupid before you find out why — that's stupid.'

Mai had hauled Finn out of the living room too. 'Brian is a guest in this house for two days. You'll make him feel welcome. I won't argue with you about this, Finn,' she said. 'It might've been my mistake in the first place, it probably was, but the boy's here now, make the best of it. And Finn —'

'Yeah, Mum,' he groaned. He knew that tone well.

'Don't forget that you and Kes are the oldest. The younger ones will follow your lead. It hasn't all been easy for Brian, either, you know. He's not as deaf as Angie, but he's been very ill over the years and he's spent far more time in hospital. Take that look off your face and put up with it. What's happened has happened.'

'Yeah, it's all right for you, you don't have to entertain him.'

'Tough. It's done. You can make it turn out all right if you try. You can head off in a minute ... and don't be rude to his mother. Just because they're ill-mannered, it doesn't mean you have to be, too. Here, have some sponge cake.'

Saturday afternoon, three o'clock. Nearly the whole day wasted. Kes, Finn and Angie hung on in desperation until Brian's parents finally took off in their BMW and were swallowed up in a dust cloud.

'Thought they'd never go.' Finn grabbed Angie by the arm, 'Come on, let's get dork-features and clear out before we have to play party games.' Angie started to protest, giggled and wiped the smile as she caught her mother's glare.

Chapter 3

From the driver's window, Kes eyed off their visitor. She was uncertain about this one. Brian looked petulant, as if he always had the best of everything, and this place didn't measure up. He was staring around as if he found the farm, with its dust and noise and heat, an alien landscape. However, Mai, who'd put in another plea for him, could be right, he might be OK. Maybe he was shy or embarrassed by his parents. Right, Mai. He looked just like any other spoilt kid to Kes, but she did have to admit, his parents would embarrass her to death, too. She'd curl up and die of shame.

Kes laughed as she saw Charlie slide out the back door and take off to the sheds at a run. Her uncle didn't look heartbroken to see the back of Brian's parents, either.

'You lot coming?' Kes looked down at Angie, Finn and Brian from the cab. 'Lagoon limo now departing. Hop up if you are.'

'On what? On the back of this thing? Are you going to drive? Can you drive this?' Brian looked worried.

'On the property. Not on the road. Yet.'

'What if you crash?'

'What d'you mean? I don't crash things. It's my truck, I drive it carefully.'

'You're allowed? Your parents let you drive?'

'Yeah, of course. You don't think I'd be sitting in here if I wasn't, do you?'

Brian shrugged his shoulders. 'OK,' he said. 'Guess you only die once.' He climbed into the back of the truck, burning his hands on the metal.

The tray was blistering hot. They had to sit on hessian bags stuffed with something hard and uncomfortable. The sides had long since rusted out and been replaced by wooden fence palings. The back window was missing completely and through it Brian watched Kes.

'Kes and Finn rescued the truck from a paddock and got it going.'

Brian, thinking about his parents, realised that Angie was speaking to him.

'It took them eleven months, the whole of this year, to rebuild it. Finn rebuilt the engine and Kes fixed up the body work.'

'What do you cart in this thing? It stinks. How old are you, anyway?' he shouted through the back window as Kes gently crunched the gears, coaxing the truck into movement.

'Fourteen. Nearly fifteen. In a few months.'

'Fourteen!' he shouted, trying to jump off, but

the truck was already moving and he bounced back against the side railing. He glared at Finn and Angie. 'It's not funny being thrown around in a bone-breaker of a truck with a kid girl driving. She's younger than me.'

'Kes is OK, Brian,' Angie replied. 'She's a good driver. The track is hopeless with the drought. The ruts are like concrete.'

'Can you drive?' asked Finn quietly, clutching the wooden sides as the potholes flung them from side to side. 'Would you like to try?'

'No. And she can't either.'

'Then I'd shut up if I were you. It's the truck that's the problem, it's got no springs, not Kes' driving. That'd be obvious to anyone.'

Angie stared at the trees wondering how she was going to mend the widening rift between Brian and the other two. She managed a fractured conversation with him, but there was an antagonistic silence between the two boys for the twenty minutes it took them to reach the waterhole.

In normal years it was a lake-sized expanse of shallow water lying about three kilometres north of the house. Over the past eighteen months of drought it had receded to less than a quarter of its size. The reed beds were high and dry, the useable water reduced to a string of pools and the deep swimming hole was surrounded now on three sides by wide sand and clay beaches, left by the still-contracting water. It was drying up so fast Kes doubted if it could last the summer. It had never shrunk this much before.

The waterhole lay between the wild foothills of the Baw Baws, which rose sharply behind it, and a flat white dolomite claypan that became a shallow swamp in winter. In wet years you couldn't tell where the waterhole finished and the swamp began. It all became one huge shallow expanse of water, home to thousands of water birds.

The swamp was dry and salty now, its parched surface criss-crossed with shrinkage cracks and the tracks of emus, roos and hopeful water birds. Only in the centre, where a subterranean spring or soak kept it damp, was the clay still soft. Anyone or anything walking across it, or digging for water, left clear footprints.

The rockface at the back of the waterhole was so steep and smooth it made a wall from which you could jump into the water. A small waterfall, funnelling water from thick bush behind, cascaded over the wall in the winter, but it always dried up by the time the weather was hot enough to enjoy lying under it. Not even a trickle ran over the rock now and it was only November.

The youngest two Martins, Jack and Jon, had rigged up a precarious flying fox made with old rope, a crate and bits of wire scavenged from the fences. It was stretched from a tree that grew out of the rock wall to a tree on the other side of the lagoon. Theoretically, it could get them from tree to tree. Usually it got them almost into the centre of the waterhole then keeled over and dumped them out. It always broke after a few good swings. They were constantly repairing and improving it with increasingly elaborate constructions.

When the truck arrived, Jack and Jon were in the middle of the billabong diving for the crate that had come apart and sunk in the deepest part. Sarah was still sitting reading in her tree.

'Those two in the water are Jon and Jack. Twins obviously,' Finn said to Brian. 'They're Kes and Sarah's brothers. They're nine. They were born with fins and wheels instead of arms and legs. Don't worry if you can't tell them apart. Even Kate, their mum, can't sometimes. Sarah's the one up in the tree with the book. Kes, Sarah and the twins are all Martins. Angie and I are Lawsons. We're cousins. Sarah!' Finn shouted. 'This is Brian.'

Brian stared at the people around the pool. They were a strange-looking bunch. Kes Martin and her twin brothers were dark skinned and dark haired. The twins, treading water in the lagoon and waving to him, were certainly identical, with curly black hair and brown eyes. He couldn't tell them apart. They looked Aboriginal, like Kes.

Angie and her cousin, Sarah, the girl in the tree, were both about twelve, and normal, white like him. Finn Lawson, with his black hair and eyes and his golden skin, looked Chinese like his mother, Mai.

Kes jumped down from the driver's seat and

laughed. 'We're a bit much when you meet us all like this for the first time. We're a funny mob. Everyone's a bit shocked at first. We are what we look like — Angie and Finn's mum is Chinese, you know that of course. Sarah, Jon and Jack and me, our dad's Koori. You haven't met my dad Patrick yet, he's somewhere up in there today.' Kes waved in the direction of the steep mountain range in front of them. 'He's chasing cattle. You'll meet him at dinner tonight, with my mum.'

'But you're all cousins,' said Brian.

'Yeah. My mum, Kate, used to be Kate Lawson. She's the sister of their father, Charlie Lawson,' said Kes, jumping into the water fully clothed. 'Don't worry about it. You'll get the hang of us in a bit.' She dived and disappeared under water.

Brian stared at her. She'd just jumped into the water with all her clothes on. She was mad.

Angie smiled at him tentatively; he looked stunned. She linked her arm in his. 'I know you can't go in swimming, but do you want to have a look around, above the waterhole? There's some good bush up there, plenty of roos and emus. The bush goes forever, right into the heart of the Baw Baws. Or if you want we could go and catch old Fred and Freda — they're our horses. They're a bit slow — well, a bit old — ancient actually, but they're still used to being ridden. They'll be hanging around the edge of the swamp here, somewhere. We could ride around the place a bit so you'll get to know where you are.'

Brian looked at her silently.

'Or we could go back and get the motorbikes; I could take you around on the bikes if you like. Can you ride a motorbike? I could dink you if you can't.'

Brian didn't know what to reply. His backside was aching from the steel tray of the truck. He'd been told to shut up by Finn, and Kes was ignoring him. He wasn't used to girls ignoring him. If the horses were anything like the truck, they'd be bone-crushers too. He couldn't ride a motorbike, he'd never even been on one, and Angie obviously could. He'd only been on a horse a couple of times and hated it, but it looked as if Angie felt at home with both bikes and horses. He wasn't about to lose face in front of them; Finn standing around watching and listening with a smirk on his face, and the twins staring at him from the water like he was a circus sideshow.

'I'll stay here for a while,' he said, sitting on the sandy beach that ran down into the water. 'Yow! That bloody truck!' he said, getting up again, 'I'll just walk around for a bit.'

He climbed around onto the smooth rocks at one end of the billabong and stood looking down at Kes and the twins in the water.

Kes wasn't like any other girl he'd ever met. The girls he knew wouldn't be caught dead acting like that, or dressing like something out of an op shop. They certainly didn't career across paddocks in an ancient truck without seats and jump into waterholes fully dressed. They lived in normal-looking families, white ones, in normal-looking houses, in a normal place, Melbourne. He understood them. With this lot, he didn't even know where to start.

They were totally different from the idealised family Angie had described so often and in such glowing detail during their long night-time conversations in hospital. Talks that seemed to go on forever until they'd be ordered back to their beds. She hadn't set out to mislead him, but they were so far from his expectations that he felt cheated. They didn't accept him, as Angie had from the first day, and they didn't measure up to Angie's portraits of them. Something wonderful, something he'd believed in for a long time, had shattered into a hundred pieces.

It was plain Kes and Finn disliked him, Finn particularly, and he didn't care if Brian knew it. He felt intrusive and unwanted. He had no idea what to talk to them about — they'd have completely different interests. They probably never came near Melbourne, stuck out in this place.

He wondered when they'd last been to a concert or seen any live music, even a movie. What could they possibly do around here? Is this what they did for kicks? Jumped into dirty-looking waterholes with their clothes on? Great! His mother's lying had got him stuck here for a whole weekend.

If it was possible, the day was getting worse by the hour, although he hadn't thought so while his mother and father were screaming at each other in the car. Brian stared at the rippling water, echoes of the terrible fight that had lasted all the way from Melbourne were swirling around and around in his head. He really thought that this morning's battle would be the final one, the finish of the Conroy family.

They'd obviously been fighting before they got in the car. His mother was sulking and his father trying to patch it up with her. The atmosphere in the car degenerated the further they got from Melbourne, until, by the time they reached the Latrobe Valley, they were tearing strips off each other again.

Her screeching that she was leaving and going to live with Johnnie, he at least listened to her and considered her needs. His father shouting that it was a great idea, and about time she got out of his life, he was sick of her tantrums and finished with her. His mother screaming about a woman called Marcia, who she knew all about. Did he think she was blind, or didn't he care? The whole of his work was talking about them. What did he have to say about her, then?

Brian had never even heard of a Marcia.

To stop it, or at least to delay the approaching death blows, he said he was going to be sick, and got out of the car on the highway near Moe. He'd refused to get back in, shouting at his father to get away, he hated them both, to leave him alone, that he was catching the train back to South Yarra. A police car stopped because his father was crawling along next to him. His parents told the police he was carsick. That was when his mother came up with the idea of getting rid of him onto the Lawsons for the weekend, so they could continue killing each other, Brian supposed, without interference from him.

This morning it had seemed like a good idea.

The images suddenly disappeared with ripples on the water's surface. He was standing on a rock beside a waterhole, in the back-blocks of the Baw Baws, with a bunch of kids he didn't know. He looked around for Angie. She was watching him from a safe distance with a puzzled frown, as if he might bite. He dropped his eyes. He had to shake off this depression. He couldn't bear to hurt Angie, she was the closest thing he'd ever come, in his mind, to having a little sister. Funny, the way he thought of her. He only saw her a few times a year, but they never stopped talking the whole time they were together, despite their age difference. It had even become a joke amongst the nursing staff. They were called 'the Blarney twins'.

Kes waded out through the shallow water towards him. She flung her wavy black hair out of her eyes and shook a flying spray of water off herself.

'That's much better,' Kes said, dipping her head again and tossing the hair off her face. 'The old truck's like an oven. There's no proper floor and the heat rolls straight off the engine over me. It's even worse on days like this. Come in, Brian. You'll turn into grease on that rock.'

'I don't know how you can drive that thing,' Brian replied.

Kes laughed, 'Well, it's better than walking.'

'I don't know about that.'

'You soon would if you lived here.'

Brian grunted.

'You can get used to anything, you know,' she said, climbing up onto the rocks beside him, 'if you have to. Or choose to. It's fantastic having my own wheels.'

'That crate!'

'Hey! That's my Rolls you're insulting. My stretch limo. Hand-built, I might add.'

He looked at her silently then turned away, staring out over the swamp. He had to get this anger down. It was his parents who were fighting, not him; he didn't have to behave the same way. He just couldn't get a grip on it. Words kept falling out of his mouth, like tears sometimes fell out of his eyes.

Two out of ten for that feeble attempt at humour, thought Kes. This one's going to be a challenge. She wasn't mad at him, but she couldn't understand what made him so snaky. Hot? Out of his depth? Maybe his hearing's still bad. It could be all or none of those things. She started again.

'It's not usually this dry. We've had a drought for two years and on top of that it's been the driest ten months on record. Everything's stopped growing, and if it's not tough enough, it's died.'

'Yes.'

'The paddocks are the worst I can ever remember, but the swamp's great when there's water in it. It's almost dried up now, but some years when it's full, there are thousands of birds on it: swans, ducks, ibises, cormorants, cranes, herons, sometimes even pelicans. It's fantastic, the swamp's black with birds.'

'If you like that Mother Nature stuff. I'd rather go clubbing.'

'Clubbing what?' Kes looked at him in horror, her mouth going before her brain, for an instant imagining him paddling across the swamp, bashing swans with a baseball bat.

He snorted. 'Night clubbing. It happens in cities, not here out in … Anyway you're too young.'

Kes felt really dumb. It took an instant for her to collect her wits. 'So are you. You've got to be eighteen.'

'I lie. I got a false ID card from a friend. He makes them on his computer. The people on the doors are too stupid to look closely.'

'You like going? You go often?' She'd try him out on his own ground.

'It's all right. Depends on the scene. What you can score.'

Was he trying to put her down again, or was she supposed to be impressed by that comment?

She looked at him and shook her head. 'You just go to score? Don't you enjoy the music? I'd love to be able to do that. We hardly ever get live Melbourne bands down here.'

'The bands are mostly losers. Try-hards. Like I said, it depends what you can score, then the worst of them sounds OK.'

Kes shook her head; he'd lost her. 'You're weird, Brian.'

He turned his back and there was a lengthening silence between them.

Kes was a bit embarrassed; she probably shouldn't have said that. 'But anyhow, it's boiling here. Do you want to go in? Finn can lend you some bathers. He chucked some in the truck for you, or you can go in your shorts, or just your jocks if you want. We all do. You could cool off even if you don't put your head under.'

'It looks dirty.'

Kes laughed. 'Oh, Brian, it's all new to you, isn't it? It's not dirty, it's got tannin in it. The leaves and bark dropping in give it that tea colour. It looks brown, but it's quite safe. The stock's fenced off from here, which is why the water stays so clear, they can't churn up the clay base under the fine sand. Mum even had it tested for *E. coli*; you can drink it if you want. We wouldn't swim here if it was polluted.'

'Oh, yeah? Well, I think I'll pass.' Brian could feel the anger growing again. She was patronising him, a black kid from the sticks talking down to him. His family could buy and sell hers a dozen times over. His family. His bloody family. Why did he have to remember them?

'I don't know. Maybe in a minute.'

'Suit yourself.' Kes was getting sick of him. 'I'm going back in. Join me if you want, you'll fry your brain standing there.' She leapt off the rock, back into the water.

Finn sighed. He'd been putting it off. Not very generous, he knew, but he'd had Brian for three hours already. Now Kes had given up, he supposed it was his turn again. Angie was climbing up on the rocks to join him, too. She looked miserable.

Brian was still annoyed with Finn for telling him off about Kes' driving. Nobody spoke to him like that, adults or kids.

'How can you stand living here?' he said, as Finn climbed the rock.

Finn inspected him. He'd been watching the conversation with Kes and he didn't feel tolerant.

'We like it here — in fact we love it.' He wondered where Brian learned this way of speaking — at school or from his choice parents. 'You couldn't buy this place from our families — not for bars of gold.'

'Bars of gold! You've got to be joking. You'd be lucky to find someone to give it to. How did you end up here? You're a hundred kilometres from nowhere. God — talk about isolated!'

Angie threw down a towel and sat on the rock next to them. 'Of course it's isolated. You can't run a cattle farm in South Yarra, you know. You can't round up cattle with trams, Brian. Get real.'

Finn ground his teeth. Be polite, he told himself, it's only two days. He's a pain, but he's a guest. Yes, Mum.

'My dad and my aunt Kate are the third generation of Lawsons to inherit this property. Our great-grandfather, Ernest James Lawson, made some money in the gold rush and thought cattle farming was less chancy than life on the diggings.'

'He'd never seen a drought like this one, that's for sure,' Angie said.

'The mining companies got here in the late 1800s and the last of the gold prospectors gave up. His mates thought he was mad when old Lawson bought this land. They said it was worthless — inaccessible wild mountains — and that he'd wasted his money. He started running cattle and we've owned this chunk of Gippsland ever since. Over a hundred years. We're the fourth generation, us kids.'

'Well, thanks for the history lesson.'

'Brian! You asked!' Angie snapped at him. 'Finn's just telling you what you asked.'

He ignored her.

'And where did old Ernest James come from — Hong Kong? Beijing?' Brian said, hating the words as soon as they were out. He sounded like his father when he started ranting about boat people.

'Glasgow, actually. It was my other great-grandfather, Hwaung Lee, Jimmy Lee, who came from Hong Kong.' Finn handled Brian as you would a strange animal. He was such a jerk.

Finn said evenly, 'Hwaung arrived about the same time as Lawson. He came to Australia for the Maldon goldfields. Lawson came from Scotland for the adventure.'

Brian tried to think of something to get him out of this hole he'd dug himself, something clever to end this confrontation, but he was lost for words. Finn kept looking at him with a steady gaze that made him uncomfortable. Brian knew he'd gone too far. He started to speak and changed his mind, trying not to see the hurt on Angie's face.

He should never have agreed to being left here, but at Moe he'd thought anything would be better than another two hours in the car. Now he was certain it was all the wrong choice; he should've insisted on going back to Melbourne. Just gone, whether they agreed or not. A weekend on his own would've been a pleasure.

Thinking about his parents only made him angrier. He tried to put them out of his mind. 'I'm going to look at the swamp,' he said abruptly, and walked off.

'Rude bastard,' said Finn, under his breath.

Angie looked worried. 'I'd better go with him. Don't you think?' She couldn't understand Brian's behaviour. Finn stopped her.

'Let him go. He's a prick. He can stew in his own bad temper for a while. He'll only upset you. If he's on his own, he might walk it off.'

'What's the matter with him? He isn't usually like

this. He's great to me in hospital. Really tries to make me laugh, keep me happy, especially last time when I was in for so long. Now he's so mad! I'll go with him, he knows me. I can talk to him — talk him around.'

'Ang!' Finn grabbed her. 'Let him go. You're too nice.'

'There's something the matter with him. I know there is. He can't just go off on his own like that, it's horrible. He'll tell me.'

'He won't. He's in a vile mood about something. Leave him, Ang. He'll chew you up and spit you out as bubbles.'

'We'll go,' said Jack, coming out of the water. 'We'll ride with him. We don't care what he says.'

'We'll go if you can bring up the flying-fox crate, Finn,' Jon bargained. 'We can't get down far enough. Jack keeps popping up. He's like a cork, it must be what he eats.'

'He's full of hot air,' said Angie, watching Brian striding out towards the swamp.

'Stale farts,' said Jon.

'We'll come with you, Brian,' shouted the twins. Brian turned around. The twins were coming after him across the swamp on two of the most ancient push-bikes he'd ever seen. One was yellow, painted with house paint; the other was completely red with rust. He looked at them in disbelief.

'Where did you get those things?' he said. 'I can't believe the wheels still turn round. You don't even have tyres.'

Jon's face lit up, 'We found 'em in the Andrews' old shearing shed. The place next door, over the back of those hills. They'd been in the shed since Mr Andrews was a kid. About forty years. They were completely covered in spider webs. You couldn't even see them; like in a horror movie. They're good, eh? We made 'em work.'

'You could at least put tyres on them.' Were they all mad in this family?

'Too many bindis for tyres,' said Jack. 'We get punctures. The wheels've had it anyway, we're saving up for new ones.'

'God, I've seen better in a tip. Horror movie's right.'

The twins looked at each other. Jack shrugged, 'It beats walking.'

'Or driving in the truck. At least your bum doesn't hurt as much,' added Jon.

'If your sister wasn't such a pathetic driver, she'd go around potholes instead of crashing through them.'

'What's the matter with you?' Jack rode in circles around him. 'She's not a bad driver. The track down here's all ruts and potholes. You have to go through 'em. What are you so mad about?'

Brian didn't know. Well, he did if he was honest,

but he wasn't about to discuss his parents with any of this crowd, especially not these two kids.

He turned around sharply. They were imitating him behind his back. Brian shouted at them.

'Piss off, the pair of you.'

'Sorry, Brian.' Jon balanced on his back wheel. 'Just kidding.'

'Piss off and leave me alone.' Christ! How was he going to get through another whole day and a half of this?

'Are you coming back to the waterhole? We need to know where you're going, in case you get lost.'

'What? Out here? Get lost? That's what you can do, the pair of you.'

'Do you want to take a bike?' asked Jack. 'You could ride back to the house.'

'Get real,' said Brian and walked off across the claypan. 'I wouldn't be seen dead on that heap of crap.'

Chapter 4

BY SIX O'CLOCK everyone was starting to worry.
Brian hadn't come back to the waterhole and
hadn't made his way to the house either. The oldest two
were in serious strife for allowing him to go off on his
own, and the younger ones had the feeling that they
were also expected to take some of the blame. Angie felt
it was all her fault, and was savage with Kes and Finn,
especially with Finn, who had stopped her going with
Brian.

Charlie, out in the farm truck, was searching the
tracks around the waterhole. Pat and Kate Martin had
the ute in the side paddocks out to the east, where they
sloped down off the plateau into gullies and down into
the Federation township.

Kes and Finn had the two motorbikes in the bush
up behind the waterhole. Sarah and Angie were walking
the edge of the claypan, and the twins were doing what
they usually did, riding their bikes into places where no
other human being would venture.

It was Sarah who, after two hours, picked up the
first signs of him. Crossing the far side of the swamp,

she and Angie cut across a person's tracks in the soft clay, heading towards the scrub on the far edge.

'Wish I knew how to track,' said Angie. 'You could tell if this was Brian or not.'

'But look, Ang!' Sarah traced around the footprint with her finger, 'it is him! You know those fancy Reeboks he had on — well look at the pattern in that print. That's his runners. I noticed them before, in the sand down by the waterhole. Look how the sole cuts right in around these curved lines, and the crosses inside those squares.'

Angie looked at her in admiration. 'Yes! You're right! Now what? Should we try to find him? His tracks are heading off towards the Number 8 bore track. Do we have time before it's dark? Maybe you should go after him. I better go back and get Dad.'

Sarah was squatting over the footprints. 'Yeah, OK. It's probably better if I chase him. You won't hear him if he answers your shouts. How deaf is he, Ang? Will he hear me if I bellow loud enough?'

'His hearing's good now. It's only been bad round the times when he's had an op. I think he'll hear you OK.'

'I'll chase him. You get Charlie. He's down by the waterhole. I can still hear the truck. We don't have much more daylight left, it's nearly half-past eight. I'll try to follow Brian as far as I can. If I find him before it gets dark, we'll come back out onto the swamp. I'll come out onto the swamp anyhow, with or without him. Look for me there.'

It was another half-hour before Angie caught up with her father. The sun was setting, dropping over the range as they jolted across the paddock to the edge of the swamp.

In the late evening light, against the golden glowing sky, they could just distinguish two figures, still about a kilometre away, emerging from the dark tree line and walking towards them.

'There they are, over the far side,' said Charlie. 'She's done it! I don't believe it. Good old Sarah!' He let out a huge sigh of relief. 'I thought we'd have the SES and the cops searching out here all night, with lights and the full catastrophe. You've done well, you two,' he said to Angie, opening the door of the truck and climbing out. 'Not that you ever should've ever let him out of your sight in the first place. You can't let city kids wander around like our mob. They get lost. Not that losing that little runt would've been such a calamity. God, what a waste of a day that was, eh Ang? But I'm sure his parents love him — they're the sort who would — and don't tell your mother I said that. We've all been in enough trouble for one day.'

Angie hugged him; he was such a comfortable father. 'I was so scared, I thought he was really lost. He's all right really, Dad. He's good to me at the hospital. No, more than that. He's great to me in hospital, like when I was crook after the last operation. We spent ages together then; he used to read me stories from this old myths and legends book he had. He'd read for hours. He was always around; said I'd run off and get lost if he didn't keep an eye on me. Funny, isn't it? He's the one who got lost.'

'Well, I'm glad he's got some saving graces … even if most of us can't see them.'

'Please don't be cross with him, Dad. Please, Dad. Please. Something's wrong and the others are being horrible to him. I don't know what's up with him. Maybe we're all just a bit too much. A bit too different.'

'You can say that again.' Charlie smiled at her. 'But I like us the way we are, Angie, black and white and yellow and brindle. He's OK by the look of things from this distance. Seems to be walking all right. We can't take the truck onto the swamp; it's too sticky in the middle. Couldn't stand bogging it tonight and we've still got to round up the rest.' He took the rifle out of its hanger and fired it into the air. 'Let everyone know we've got the little bugger.'

Brian was very subdued when they all met up in the middle of the claypan.

'You've led us in a few circles, young man. We've all been out searching for you for hours,' said Charlie severely. 'You don't wander off like that on your own if you don't know the country. But you've been lucky this time and you've got Sarah to thank for that; you could be spending the night out there. It looks as if a couple of scratches are the worst you've suffered.'

He smiled at his niece. 'You did very well, Sarah. Angie said you tracked him down.'

'It's those runners he's wearing. They give a clear sole print. I could follow them for ages across the clay and then I picked them up again on the sand track running out to the old Number 8 bore. He was wandering around out there, thinking he was going towards the house, but still walking completely in the wrong direction, heading for Mansfield, I think.'

'Thanks for finding me,' Brian mumbled. 'I'm sorry.' He was very tired and looked acutely embarrassed. He was badly scratched around the arms and legs and had an insect bite over one eye that had swollen, partly closing it.

'I got turned around. I was sure I was going back to the waterhole. I couldn't recognise anything; it all looks the same out there, that scrubby stuff. A couple of hours ago I found the swamp again and I thought I knew the way. Then I heard Sarah calling. That was a pretty good sound. I thought I'd be walking all night. Here,' he said suddenly, 'you have this.'

He pulled something large and dark-green out from under his jacket and held it out to Sarah. It was an emu egg. 'All the others had hatched and were staggering around. The adult bird drove me off, but I managed to get this one. I was going to take it home, but you can have it.'

Angie's heart sank. The egg would have hatched if he'd left it. She looked at Sarah, who was holding the egg and gazing at Brian in disbelief. 'You took this from a nest? It's ready to hatch! You've probably killed it!'

She started to shout, anger rising in her. 'You idiot! Don't you know anything?'

'Enough, Sarah,' said Charlie. 'He's had enough for one day. We all have. It's getting dark. We'll never find the nest now. Brian didn't know — well, he didn't think. Come on, we have to get back, we're running out of light and I still have stuff to do with the cattle. I'll be working half the night in the dark as it is.'

Angie held out her hand for the egg. 'Can I try, Sarah? Can I try to hatch it? It's still warm and Brian's had it under his shirt. Can you hear anything in it? Hold it up to your ear. I read that you can tell when they're nearly ready to hatch, you can hear them.'

'You can hear chickens. Charlie, can Angie use the incubator? If it's going to hatch — if he hasn't killed it already — it'll hatch there,' she said, giving Brian another dirty look.

'Sure,' said Charlie, 'but don't be disappointed if it doesn't work. It's a bit of an uphill battle with the last egg to hatch, in the best of circumstances. They're usually the weakest of the brood. Come on now, you lot, pile in the back. We have to get back and round up the rest of the tribe, they'll be halfway to New South Wales by now, and God only knows where the twins will've got to. Queensland, probably. Angie, if you're going to carry that egg, get up in front with me.'

Angie set up the incubator as soon as she got home. The great green egg, as large as her cupped hands, lay in the straw under the warming light bulb and did nothing. Sarah said she could hear a sound, but no one else could.

Dinner was tense. Brian was silent, replying only in monosyllables to questions he was asked directly. His face was set in an unhappy scowl and his fists clamped so tightly in his lap that Angie, sitting next to him, could see the veins sticking out of the back of his hands. It was impossible to tell if he was ashamed about the trouble he'd caused or angry with everyone, but those who had been out searching for him for hours were tired and by the end of dinner they couldn't care less how Brian felt.

Mai, forever kind, kept trying to find something that would spark his interest. Angie managed to squeeze some conversation out of him, but everyone was glad when the meal was over.

Angie climbed into bed still in her jeans and T-shirt. Poor old Finn had Brian in his room, which she knew he'd hate. As soon as her parents had gone to bed, she climbed out her window and raced down to the hatching shed. She curled up next to the incubator on a heap of new straw and watched the great egg lying under the warm yellow glow. She was determined to stay awake all night to watch the egg hatch, but the day had tired her out and she fell asleep within minutes.

She woke with a start an hour later. The egg was

exactly the same. During the rest of the night she dozed and woke startled each time, wondering where she was and what on earth she was doing on an itching pile of straw in the hatching shed.

At four o'clock, just as it started to get light, Angie woke again. A tiny hole had appeared in the end of the egg and the hard little beak end of the emu chick was cracking its way out.

What a shock you have in store for you, Angie thought. I don't look much like a mother emu, sorry bird. I'll look after you though.

The chick struggled out of its huge egg, beak and feet first, and fell in a messy, striped heap onto the straw, all head, eyes and legs. Angie was enchanted.

She had no idea what to feed it, but thought that if it was to survive on a chook farm it might be a good idea for it to get used to chicken feed. She made up a wet mash used for the newly hatched chicks and fed the baby bird off her finger. To her surprise and delight, the little creature crammed it down. Angie was afraid of it overeating and took the dish away, but it struggled to its feet and wobbled after the plate. Angie picked the wet chick up and cuddled it.

By six o'clock, when people started appearing in the yard, the tiny striped chick was dry, fluffy and following Angie's feet wherever she moved. Angie had never seen anything so beautiful.

Sarah was equally taken by the chick. Together they spent hours crawling around in the garden with it.

They named it, male or female, sex yet unknown, Emma the emu.

Brian slept very little that night. By morning his bed was twisted into a knotted mess of sheets. He found it impossible to disengage his mind from the questions that had haunted his sleep. What would happen to him when his parents split up? Who'd he live with? Where'd that be? He was never going to live with his mother's boyfriend, Johnnie, he loathed him, but he fought with his father most of the time, more and more, the older he got. And anyhow, now there was this Marcia person. Where was she going to fit into the picture? He wasn't going to stay around if she moved in when his mother moved out.

Maybe they'd make him become a boarder, but he had no friends among them; they were a tight, exclusive gang. But then if his parents split up, maybe there wouldn't be enough money for him to board, or even stay at school. And did that mean his house would be sold to split up the money? Would he have to move, start at a new school in a new suburb?

Finn's bed squeaked, and every time Brian drifted off, Finn's movements woke him. There were no answers in the night, just restless tossing and escalating problems.

The birds woke him again at dawn and he lay quietly trying to imagine that his parents had sorted out their feud and that life would go on as normal, but it was the worst fight he'd ever heard, and he didn't think a weekend away would help. If anything, just the two of them being in each other's company for two days, would cement the chasm between them.

On top of all that, he was bitterly sorry about yesterday. He was ashamed of the way he'd behaved to Finn and Kes, ashamed of getting lost, and even taking the emu egg had turned out to be wrong.

He got up, determined to make up for yesterday, but there seemed to be an impassable barrier between him and the others now. They were distant, talked politely to him, and left him alone more and more as the day passed. Only Angie gave him anything more than the briefest attention, and she was so taken by the emu chick that she was barely aware of anything else.

Kes found him about four o'clock that afternoon, sitting on the veranda staring into space. She felt guilty that she hadn't tried harder with him.

'Do you want to come out with me in the truck and have a look in the other direction? You probably know the swamp well enough by now,' she laughed.

Brian raised his head. Kes stared. He'd been crying.

'You'd even get to sit up front. Not that the passenger seat is exactly luxurious, but it's stuffed with old rags at least, not sawdust like the bags on the back.'

Brian looked baffled, as if he'd been asked a question that was too hard to answer.

'Come on. There's a whole lot of tracks up here on the plateau that head over to the escarpment behind

Federation. Federation's interesting, but I can't take you down there, not on public roads. There's an old gold mining area over to the east, Piper's Mine, that's got some good stuff in it, it's never been vandalised. Not many people know about it, it's still on our property. Come on, your parents could be ages yet.'

Brian followed her to the truck. He's probably going to enjoy this about as much as I will, Kes thought, but at least Ang will quit eating me for lunch.

'We start on the entrance track, then we take off up that hill.' Kes pointed to a steep knoll over to the south-east that ended in cliffs rising to the eastern horizon. 'It'll be a bit bumpy.'

'It's OK. I won't break.'

It was an awkward couple of hours. After the first half-hour, Kes found it hard to keep up a conversation. Brian kept drifting off, staring out the window with a blank face. He asked a few polite questions about the tracks that ran around the edge of the valley, but the only animation she could get from him was when they talked about Angie. It was clear that Brian really cared for her, something which Kes found at odds with his off-hand behaviour to the rest of them.

They left the truck on the edge of the plateau and headed further up the valley wall to Piper's Mine. It was on a ledge at the base of a cliff, tunnelled into the cliff face, only reachable by a climb, hand over hand, on slippery shale. The loose rock slipped away under their feet as they scrambled up the last hundred metres.

Most people were swept away by the view and the eyrie home that the old miner had created. Two slab huts, shaded by stunted eucalypts, were perched on a grass-covered ledge about twenty metres wide. The flat around the huts was covered in white and pink everlastings and blue-grey tussock grass. Two ravens sat on the roof, scolding the intruders.

The mine, dug deep into the cliff, was cool and dark inside.

'Is it safe? What about cave-ins?' Brian strained to see into the blackness, blinded by the bright sunlight.

'With our parents! Dad has the mining inspector up here every year. He's paranoid about old mines. Convinced they're going to jump out of the ground and swallow us!'

Their eyes slowly grew used to the dark.

'It's not very long, only about forty metres, but every bit of it's been picked out by hand through solid rock. He must've been a toughy, old Piper.'

After an initial burst of enthusiasm, Brian didn't seem particularly interested in the mine, or the old huts, or their bush furniture made from gnarled trees and kerosene tins. Kes made most of the conversation. The view over the Federation valley was stunning, the sky brilliant blue, and a sea of hills receded to the far horizon in waves of golden green and smoky blue.

Kes could sit and stare at it for hours. She felt like her namesake up here; as if she could spread her wings and take off from this ledge, soaring on the thermals above the mountains.

Brian sat beside her on a rough bench. Kes pointed out the gold-mining structures of Federation spread out below them, the remains of the huge water wheel, the poppet head and the battery. She traced the track that the original miners had followed up the river and into Gloriana Creek. There, the lucky early ones had found huge deposits of alluvial gold. The later ones had carved out water races, tunnelled into the hill and established the original shantytown.

'It used to have a population of 34,000! It was built all along one side of Front Street, then spread up into these hills. The tourist signs say that "Gloriana Creek's golden gravel made the fortunes of the first miners and broke the backs of the latecomers." Like old Piper. He never found a trace in this tunnel.'

Kes picked out the blue, domed roof of the deserted Palace Hotel. 'See that row of windows just under the roof? The ones shining in the sun? Those were the tiny bedrooms for the dancing girls. They still have their original furniture. The more popular girls had their clothes and furniture brought in on bullock teams from Melbourne. Must have cost a fortune.'

Kes had been inside the Palace several times and liked to kid herself that if she listened to its walls she could hear the sounds of the girls' feet dancing to the tinny piano.

'The inside's still the same as it was a hundred years ago,' she told Brian. 'It's got this faded flowery wallpaper in panels between massive gold-framed mirrors. The mirrors reach from floor to roof and they're all dark and spotted with age. There's a tiny stage with heavy green brocade curtains on fat brass rods. Everything's quietly turning to dust.'

It was the dust that fascinated Kes most. It smelt old and still. She wondered if the place had ever been cleaned since it was closed up, or was the bottom layer of dust the one that had settled seventy-five years ago? The wooden furniture and the ornate bar were older, but the dust was somehow more human. Had it come from old dresses, feather hats and boas? From the dirt road outside? Did the stamping feet billow it around in clouds before it finally settled here?

Kes glanced at Brian. She couldn't tell if he was interested or lost in his own world. 'The locals say that the ground under the bar was so rich with the gold dust which fell though the floorboards that it was panned.'

Brian seemed anxious to get back to the house. He kept looking at his watch and seemed relieved when they headed down off the ridge and back to the truck.

'Did the height worry you?' Kes asked as she coaxed her truck into firing. 'Gill, my best friend from school, she can't cope with it up there. I have to hold her hand the whole time. She loves it, but she can't cope with the height.'

'No. I was fine.'

'I thought you might've wanted to come down.'

'No, I was fine. Heights don't bother me.'

Kes had completely run out of conversation by the time they got back.

'My parents aren't here yet,' Brian said, as they stopped in the yard. 'It's after six.'

'You can have dinner with us.'

'It's not that. They're just — late, that's all.'

Finn was carrying a bucket of feed to the chook sheds. He raised his hand and waved.

'Don't worry about Finn,' Kes said apologetically, 'or any of us. He doesn't mean to be … we don't mean to be unfriendly. We're just a bit — different. Finn's OK really.'

'It's not you. Finn, or any of you,' he replied, getting out and walking towards the house. 'It's me,' he mumbled, beyond her hearing.

'Well thanks for the grand tour! So interesting! Such great company,' Kes said, under her breath, as he walked off. She felt as if she'd been slapped in the face.

Brian's parents didn't arrive until nearly ten. They gave no reason for being so late, barely stayed long enough to thank Mai for having their son, and said nothing to anyone else.

Finn, Sarah and Kes said awkward goodbyes.

Angie gave Brian a brief hug and got a fleeting smile in reply, then they were gone.

'I won't cry buckets if I never see him again,' Kes said, as soon as Angie was out of sight.

'I'm going to bed,' said Finn.

Chapter 5

LIKE MANY CREATURES raised by humans from birth, the emu chick decided Angie was its parent, but in the first few days of its life she confused the tiny creature. The chick obviously didn't care what its parent looked like — Angie's shape would do fine — but Kes told them Angie would also have to sound right. Sarah coached Angie, who had never heard the deep booming sound of an emu, until she became a passable emu parent. From that time on, Emma never left the back of her legs. The chick followed her all day calling with a particularly anxious and penetrating beep if Angie left her sight for a second. At night, she slept in a basket beside Angie's bed. When Emma was old enough to discover that Angie slept in the bed above her, she'd scramble around the room, jumping onto boxes and bookshelves until she could scrabble her way up onto the bed, nesting down between Angie's feet and the wall.

Mai and Charlie stood watching their sleeping daughter one night. Emma squatted on Angie's stomach, her long neck draped across Angie's chest, and her bill tucked tenderly into Angie's neck.

Mai shook her head. 'The girl's raising a monster. Can you imagine what we'll have in a few months with a full-grown emu trying to sleep on top of that child?'

It was lucky that the rest of the Lawson family shared some of Angie's love of the bird. Angie's bedroom showed clear signs of inadequately cleaned up emu poo and smelt like a chook pen.

During November, things became even more difficult on the property. Gippsland had already suffered a year of severe drought. Another dry winter, followed by the El Niño, forecast disaster and brought drought from Queensland to Victoria for a second year. Most of the property's artesian springs had stopped running as the water table dropped. Two of the bores had run dry and others were erratic.

By the end of November there had still only been patchy spring rain, wrecking the growing season and producing a sparse cover of grass — just enough to keep the already diminished cattle numbers at subsistence level. With two bad years in a row, another sale of cattle at rock-bottom prices was inevitable. If there was no rain before Christmas, the breeding stock would have to be reduced again to bare essentials.

Sarah was developing a new passion. After her success at finding Brian, she was determined to teach herself to track. With her mind set on something, she was like a dog with a bone, single-minded to the point of provoking screaming exasperation in the rest of the family.

It had been that way with her trumpet. No one in either house would ever forget the weekend Sarah learned to play. First she was banished from the kitchen to her room, then to the yard, then to the hay-shed, then to the far end of the home paddock, but at the end of the weekend — 'A very long weekend,' said her mother — Sarah could play the thing. She worked at it until she became proficient; not brilliant, and not with the ease with which Finn could pick up a new instrument, but well able to keep her place in the school orchestra, even as a beginner in Year 7.

About a week after Brian left, Sarah was walking across the swamp with Kes and their parents. They had been out to the old Number 4 bore on the far side of the claypan, to see if it could be reactivated without costing a fortune. The answer was, unfortunately, no. The windmill was still in good condition, but the state of the bore below ground level was beyond hope.

In previous years, there had been no need for this bore which, temperamental at the best of times, had fallen into disuse. The internal casing below ground was rusted out and the bore-hole was collaps-ing in on itself. Nothing short of a complete re-drill would sort it out.

On the way home across the swamp, they

crossed Brian's footprints heading out away from the homestead.

'Here are the tracks of that idiot. I should've left him in the bush,' said Sarah.

'Sarah! That's horrible,' said Kate.

'Yeah, Mum, you didn't have to put up with him all weekend.'

'Sarah!'

'He was, Mum. You didn't see half of what we had to put up with. Bet you didn't know he had some funny-looking tablets in his Calvin Klein matching bags. Did you? He tried to pretend to Finn that they were something exotic. It was probably Panadol. For his poor precious ears. The ones that are going to be school captain or prime minister next year, even though they've got tubes in them.'

Kate laughed in spite of herself. 'Charming child, you are! I'm glad you lot are all so perfect.'

'Perfect treasures we are, Mum,' said Sarah. 'Don't you forget it. Appreciate us while you can. Before I run away and marry Brian. No, Kes can. Nice rich boy, lovely parents! I think he liked Kes, he kept an eye on her. Well, he kept trying to impress her. And Kes took him out riding all by herself!'

'Oh yeah,' Kes said, 'I was totally dazzled.'

'He must've felt really uncomfortable being dumped here like that without warning for a whole weekend. Poor little devil, he had to put up with you lot, too, don't forget. You especially, Sarah, you never gave him an inch. Angie and Kes were the only ones who tried,' Kate said.

'He was a real idiot, Mum,' Sarah fired back. 'Right off the scale on my crap detector. Don't make excuses for him. Some people just are, and he was.'

'Yeah, I wasn't too impressed,' said Pat. 'I won't lose much sleep if I never see him again.'

'Well, you know what Mai's like,' said Kate. 'She'd bring home every lame dog in Gippsland if she could. Angie's the same.'

A few hundred metres further on they picked up Sarah's track, widely spaced.

'Look, you've been running,' said Pat. 'Your toes are dug in and the footprints are spaced out.'

'Over here,' called Kes. 'Angie's prints are here with yours now, Sarah.'

'That's where we stood and talked. Look — the toes are even pointing at each other. We should find — yes, look there. That's when Angie left to get Charlie. Here, she's started running too. It's a story printed in clay, like those old Egyptians and their clay tablets. The footprints are so clear you should still be able to hear us talking, as if the words are still hanging around here somewhere in the air.'

Sarah was quiet for a time, getting down on her hands and knees to look intently at the eroded prints of swamp emus and roos.

'You'll find all Emma's aunts and uncles there,'

called Kes, 'but I still can't believe Brian took that egg,' she added to her father. 'What an idiot! Emma's lucky, though. She's found herself a good mother in Angie.'

'Father,' said Pat. 'The father looks after the chicks. Like me. Good emu dad.'

'Dad,' called Sarah, running to catch up with them, 'will you teach me how to track? Properly, I mean. Like Kooris track.'

'Seems to me you're pretty good already. You followed that bloke for more than a kilometre by my calculations.'

'No. Properly! You know how a good tracker can see signs that are invisible to us. You know what I mean. Not just down sand tracks and across damp claypans, anyone can do that.'

Pat smiled at his daughter's eager face. 'I was brought up in Melbourne, I never learned anything like that. Wish I had, but I didn't even see bush until I was a teenager and went to work on a farm.'

'But what about when you were a young kid. You weren't born in Melbourne.'

Kes glanced quickly at her father. She knew little of his early life, but she did know it had been unhappy. She saw his face grow distant for a moment.

'No. I was taken to Melbourne when I was very young. Two, I think. I can hardly remember — well, I can vaguely remember two people before that, I think one was my mother and one was my aunt or someone close to me. I didn't see them again after I went to Melbourne.'

'Why?' said Sarah. 'Did they die or something?'

'No. I don't think so. I don't know. Maybe.'

'What do you mean, you don't know?' cried Sarah. For the first time in her life she realised that her own father had grown up without knowing anything at all about his parents. 'I suppose I knew you'd been brought up at that home place, but I didn't know you didn't ever see your parents. Why didn't you see them again? You can't just lose you parents! Can you?' She looked anxious.

Kate said, 'We won't lose anyone if you learn to track.'

'But where are they? Where did they go?' Sarah persisted.

'Sarah, I don't know, and I don't know why. Things were different in those days. A lot of kids were taken away from their families and brought into the cities. The Government thought it would give Aboriginal kids a better chance in life.'

'Better? Better than what?' said Kes, immediately sensing an injustice to her father.

'Than growing up in the outback in what the Government thought were poor and dirty conditions.'

'You mean like us here?' asked Sarah.

'We might be poor but we're not all dirty. Your father and I are quite clean, thank you,' laughed Kate.

'The twins aren't. They're always covered in something disgusting.'

'Better than growing up with your mum and dad, did they mean? They really thought living in an orphanage was better?' asked Kes.

'Things were different then,' said Pat.

'Where were you born?' Sarah stood in front of him demanding answers. 'You've never told us about any of this. What happened? You can't just get posted somewhere. Kids aren't parcels you know, Dad!'

'I don't know. My birth certificate only gives the orphanage where I was raised. And no,' he added, smiling at his daughter's angry face, 'it doesn't say who my parents were. I was renamed Patrick John Martin after I reached there.'

'But you weren't an orphan. Or maybe you weren't an orphan. Someone must know how you got there, who you really are,' Sarah said.

Pat stopped. He looked at the wide sweep of the horizon, the shades of deepening blue of the hills rolling away into the Baw Baws, and the single eagle hunting over them. His eyes grew sadder than Kes had ever seen them.

Sarah shouted at her father, 'You must know who you are! Everyone does. You're not — not — an emu chick. You couldn't have been just picked up and taken away like Emma. You must know who you are.'

'I know,' said Kate. 'He's the father of two very inquisitive girls who are late for feeding the chooks, so come on, step on it.' She took Sarah's hand and walked her off ahead.

Kes, not so easily put off, linked her arm in her father's and lagged behind deliberately. 'Don't you wish you knew?' she asked quietly.

He hesitated before answering her and she saw that hurt in his eyes again. 'Many times, Kes, but that was the way of the world then. I'm not going to ruin my happiness with Kate and you kids now, by crying over past wrongs and things I can't change. And I can't change losing my family when I was two.'

'Have you ever tried to find them?'

'I did. When I was a lot younger. I tried several times. The last time was when Kate and I got married. They wouldn't tell you anything in those days.' He paused. 'I don't know, Kes. Maybe they're all dead. Maybe they don't want to know about me. Maybe they haven't tried either.'

'Maybe they didn't know where to start either, you mean.'

He put his arm around her. 'Other things become more important in the end, Kes. Kate. You kids. All our mob. This place. I'm just so incredibly lucky to have all this, sometimes I think I'd be pushing my luck beyond breaking point if I had more.'

'You got your brolga back. That's more.'

'Yes, about time, you thieving magpie,' he said, smacking her gently.

But Kes made up her mind right then, that one day she'd find her father's family. She'd keep it a secret until she had the answer. One day, she'd give it to him as a present.

Chapter 6

DURING THE 1930S depression, when the bottom dropped out of the cattle market, Charlie and Kate's father, Kenneth Lawson, built chook sheds and began breeding chooks to feed his family. The number of birds on the farm went up and down according to the fortunes of the family. With cattle prices down again and two bad seasons in a row, they were now vital.

'Without those chooks,' Kate said, whenever the kids complained about feeding them, 'we'd be even more broke. So get yourself down there, feed them, and try and feel grateful to them while you're at it.'

During the last two hot nights when she couldn't sleep, Kes had been planning. She went searching for Finn who was out in one of the worksheds near the hay storage. She pushed her way through the cattle hanging around the door waiting and hoping for a handout of feed.

Finn was building a box on wheels, every hammer stroke shifting ancient dust that filtered down from the rafters in stripes of shimmering sunlight. This was the original split-slab shed that had been the first building on the property 120 years ago. Their great-grandparents lived in it for years before their fortunes turned and they had enough money to build the two houses that the Martins and Lawsons now occupied. These days it was the dumping place for all the farm equipment that their great-grandparents and grandparents had used and no one wanted to throw out. Sickles, scythes, hand forged chains and brass harnessing gear. Old wooden carpentry tools, shafts and wheels from horse-drawn carts, an ancient hand-pump that still worked, the first telephone the farm ever owned with its heavy hand piece and massive battery in a wooden box. Buckets, dippers and candlesticks hand-made on the farm in the time of their great-grandparents, old oil lights, probably worth a fortune in Melbourne, hanging in a row down the ridge pole, and two walls of useful bits and pieces in oily wooden boxes with brass handles.

'What are you doing?' The workshop bench was cluttered with bits of pipe, rods, wood and wheels.

'It's for the twins. They want a contraption they can drag around behind their bikes. I don't know what's going to come to grief first, them or the bikes. The bikes aren't exactly high-tech. This thing'll pull them apart.'

'Better not let them hear you. They've never forgiven Brian for calling their bikes a heap of crap.'

'Oh yeah,' he said, squatting back on his toes,

smiling up at her. 'The horrible Brian. We who are so perfect.'

'No one who stuffs away the quantity of mangoes you do could ever get close to it, so don't pretend you're suddenly so sophisticated and tolerant and above it all. I saw you get aggro with him, too.' She pushed him off balance and he rolled in the dust, laughing. 'And you didn't take him out riding in the truck, I noticed.'

'Me, so perfect. The perfect mango consumer. That's me.'

'Perfect idiot, I reckon. Get up and listen to me. I've got an idea and I've got to talk to you about it, because you've got to be part of it.'

'Go, Kes!' He wiped the dust out of his eyes on his torn T-shirt.

Kes jumped up to sit on the old slab workbench. Finn watched her, silhouetted against the window translucent with red dust, her face alight with a new plan. He realised he'd seen her like this hundreds of times, from the time they were toddlers — Kes dragging him off somewhere by his shirt, her face sparkling, to get involved in some new and exciting scheme.

'Well, you know how hard the drought's going to hit this summer. They're saying it'll be worse even than last year. I don't know what's going to happen with the cattle going downhill the way they are. I know the olds are more worried than they'll say.'

'I know they are too, it's so annoying the way they treat us like a little kids. Here, lean on the end of the rod; I have to drill it. It's such a dumb act. Mum even stopped talking yesterday when I came in. Pathetic. They must think we can't read the paddocks. Can't see the cattle are skin and bone.'

Finn slipped the drilled rod through the piping and attached wheels with a split pin. 'Voilà! Back wheels! Disaster number 476 on track for a smashing finish.'

'Brilliant. You can start on some suspension for the truck. That could do with a touch of the old Finn genius. Anyway, we can't do much about rain, but I'm wondering if we, you and me, could do something with the chooks. I was thinking that maybe we could work up the breeding stock with a good eating bird. By March or April of next year we could have some ready to sell.'

'On top of the eggs we already sell, and those few table birds?'

'Yeah. It might help a bit next year until we get rain and the cattle build up again. What d'you think?'

'It's a heap of work, but I suppose we've only got a few weeks of school left.' Finn was measuring the pipe for the front wheels. 'There's much more work in it than just sending out eggs. You know our mums used to do dressed carcasses, but they stopped most of it because of the time involved.'

'That's when we were all little. You and I'd be the

bodies doing the cleaning, plucking and packing, all that stuff.'

'You'll never get Angie or Sarah to help. They won't kill birds now they've got Emma, they're almost vegos.'

'I know. It'd be up to us. They're too young anyhow, they'd lose interest after a week.'

'I'll do it if you reckon it's worth it. We'll have to work it out with Kate, about costs for feed and transport.' Finn jumped up. 'It'd be great if it worked. Anything that works has gotta be better than hanging around helpless.'

After a long family discussion, Kate, in charge of the property's accounts, decided it was worth a try, particularly if the breeding stock was increased to a larger size beyond the initial trial batch of a hundred birds.

'So now you can stop treating us like little kids,' said Finn. 'It's obvious the farm's in trouble, so stop trying to hide it.'

Mai, disconcerted, said, 'It's not that we think of you as children, we don't want you worrying.'

'Come on, Mum! We worry more about what you're trying to hide. We'd have to be walking around with our eyes shut and fingers in our ears not to see what's happening.'

'I suppose we were trying to preserve your childhood or something.'

'That's what we mean, Mum. It's really dumb. Just don't, OK?' said Finn.

It was a long time since either he or Kes had felt like a child.

Kes and Finn set up the incubators, cleaned out and laid cut straw in a hatching shed. A fortnight later they started with the hundred fertilised eggs that in three weeks were going to hatch into their first batch of table-quality hens.

Finn and Kes were extraordinarily proud.

During November, Kes quietly began to chase up her father's early history. All she knew was his given name, that he'd grown up in the Whitehills Orphanage in Melbourne and that at age fifteen he'd been sent to work on a farm in Wangaratta, which he ran away from.

Her first letter to the Whitehills Orphanage was returned from the Blackburn Post Office. The orphanage had closed long ago. Kes rang the church offices in Melbourne and struggled to find anyone who'd talk to her, let alone help. No one there knew where the old records were kept, or if they still existed. Someone told her to write to a Miss Hatty in archives, but thought the records had been burnt in a fire at the orphanage.

Kes looked at the growing pile of papers covering her bed. No one wanted to tell her anything. The only person who sounded interested was a journalist from the *Age* who had replied to her inquiry about finding information from old newspapers. The *Age* wanted to send out a reporter to interview Pat. Kes was horrified. She rang the journalist back straight away. He was very difficult to put off, could obviously smell a good story, and kept tempting her with the possibility of information that they might be able to unearth. She hoped like hell that he wouldn't start ringing again.

Her hands trembled slightly as she read the reply from this morning's mail. It was from Miss Hatty, who worked in the church archives, Collins Street, Melbourne.

> Dear Miss Martin,
>
> In reference to your inquiry of the 14th November, this office can find no record of a Patrick John Martin, in care at Whitehills Orphanage in the time period you describe.
>
> The orphanage was closed in 1978 but most of the records were destroyed in the fire that burnt out the main building in 1976.
>
> Yours truly,
> Madeline Hatty

It was the handwritten P.S. which shook Kes' confidence.

I am assuming by your handwriting and the nature of your inquiry that you are quite a young person, and possibly lack guidance, otherwise I would not be taking this trouble to communicate with you.

I must point out to you that it is <u>most</u> inappropriate of you to be attempting to trace your father's family. Not only is this information legally confidential, but you are involving yourself in something which is <u>none</u> of your business.

I do not know if your family is aware of what you are doing, or whether this is some school project, or just idle curiosity on your part, but I am <u>strongly</u> suggesting to you that you do not pursue this inquiry. I assure you it is <u>quite</u> pointless. If, in fact, this is a school project, please request your teacher to communicate with me <u>immediately</u>.

Have you considered, for instance, that it is very likely that your father does not want to have contact with his original family, or they with him, on the slim chance they still exist or remember him?

Kes was more shaken by the venom of the written attack than she wanted to admit, especially the underlined words, which seemed to spit anger at her from each page.

She shuffled through the other letters that had been slowly coming back.

Dear Miss Martin — no record ... Dear Miss Martin — wrong place ... Dear Miss Martin — so sorry — we suggest — have you tried? ... Good luck with your search but ...

Miss Hatty's animosity sat on her shoulder and whispered in her ear.

Dear Miss Martin — get lost ... Dear Miss Hatty — get nicked ...

She hadn't really considered the possibility that her father mightn't want to know his family history. But he had told her clearly that he didn't want old wrongs to destroy his present happiness. She shifted around uncomfortably on the bed and rubbed her feet on Blue's back. What was she getting herself into? She turned the brown, creased photograph her father had shown her over and over, worrying at the problem but finding no answers. It was the only record Pat had of himself from the days at the orphanage. Two lines of young Aboriginal children squinted into the sun, veiled white nurses stood at the end of each row. Someone had written on the back, 'Pat Martin, sixth from left, front row.'

The photo always made Kes cry. He was the youngest child in the photo, and looked no more than three. At least the little boy next to him had his arm around him. Who was he? Friend? Cousin? Was it a casual gesture for the camera, or was it a bond that meant more? Her dad didn't know, the boy was moved again before Pat was old enough to remember. He had no memory of kindness from that period.

Kes could almost hear Madeline Hatty cackling to herself in her room full of decaying archives.

Kes wiped at her eyes and stared at her own messy room. She needed to vacuum. She had to mend that shirt for Ang; she'd been asking her for weeks. She wanted to paint her walls. Blue jumped on her bed and Kes wound her arms around her.

Perhaps she was wrong to go behind her dad's back, but the memory of his face that day on the swamp kept coming back to her. It was haunting her so much that she'd started seeing the hurt in his eyes all the time, even when he was laughing. The only time it was ever totally gone was when he was cuddling Kate or one of the kids.

Eventually, her feeling that a great injustice had been done to her father overcame her shaken confidence. She wiped her nose on Blue's back and stuffed the letters and photograph back into her storage box.

She wasn't ready to talk to Finn about what she was doing but the next day at school she told her year coordinator about the search and her dilemma. He suggested she ring the regional Aboriginal Cooperative and gave her a contact name, a Ms Bannock, who had spoken at the school last term.

Chapter 7

ONE HOT DAY in December, just before the end of the school year, Rose Bannock, the Education Liaison Officer from the Aboriginal Cooperative came to the school to meet Kes. Rose was a fantastic woman with a wide smile and a great laugh. She knew far more about Whitehills than Kes' father. It had become notorious as its history became public, before it closed in 1978.

Rose laughed away barriers that to Kes had seemed insurmountable. She talked to Kes about 'freedom of information', and of records that had long been locked away that could now be accessed by Koori people. She told Kes about Link-Up, the Aboriginal organisation that helps broken families reunite and stolen children trace their homes. Rose certainly knew that the records from the orphanage were intact, because she'd used them a year ago for a similar search. The only records burnt were to do with administration. No children's records had been touched.

Miss Hatty was lying.

Kes was silent that afternoon on the bus home. The thoughts confronting her were almost overwhelming.

Down the front, the twins were the centre of attention as usual — the bus clowns. Even the driver cracked up sometimes. Jon was pretending to be his class teacher and Jack was mimicking the headmistress, telling him off. Seb McLaren, their nearest neighbour, was being their flamboyant art and drama teacher. They had the front half of the bus stitched up.

Kes watched them, distracted. A month ago, she'd have been right into it. She could do a mean interpretation of the savage school cleaner, who told everyone off, even the Head. Today, the words, 'They don't know … they don't know anything. They're just kids,' kept running through and through her brain like a cracked record.

Kes wasn't sure, either, if she wanted them to know; they were so light-hearted, such children. It was as if she was being driven across some dividing line, like the watershed ridge behind the lagoon. On one side the water ran back into her childhood, on the other it rushed into adulthood, carrying her along in its flood.

Kes leaned her head against the window and watched the trees whizzing past. She'd spent most of the afternoon with Rose Bannock and felt wrung out, glad that there were only a few more days left in the school year. She needed time on her own to think, or maybe that was the last thing she needed. What she wanted was her best friend, Gill Papadopolous, to come back from Greece. She wanted to be able to sit down and talk to her for hours without drawing breath. She needed to test the truth of this worry, by saying it aloud.

She needed something that would bring her back to normality. Christmas and the chook project would do that, she hoped.

Kes sighed. She couldn't shake this feeling that she'd been irresponsible, that she should've known more about her father's people. She could almost physically feel the rush into adulthood beginning. As if she was driving the old truck down into Federation with no one to guide her, with her eyes shut. Her head suddenly felt light and she shook herself. That was getting a bit over-dramatic, she thought. When Finn asked what was up, Kes snapped at him, and told him to mind his own business. She stared out the bus window. He was Chinese, what would he know?

Kes couldn't believe she'd thought that! Finn, her best mate. Shit! She must be going mad! Tears sprang to her eyes and the trees swam in a watery soup.

'Don't worry about me,' she said grumpily, 'I'm having a shit of a day.'

Finn ignored her and went on talking to Shelley, the girl in front of him.

That night Kes wrote a long letter to Gill.

Dear Gill,

Talk about the life of the rich and famous! Slacking around on your Greek mountainside, being waited on by your granny while we're still being punished with exams, (actually we just finished them this morning). They weren't too bad and so far I've passed the two I know about. Guess what? I came top in Biology!! Finn's passed everything so far, brilliantly, of course. He's such a brain, top in Maths again, he makes me sick. Ang and Sarah had their first lot of real Year 7 exams, too. They don't know what's hit them, poor little buggers.

By the way, if Finn hasn't written to you yet (slacker), he's moping around the place looking all lovelorn and howling at the moon. I think he's started to read Mills and Boon. You better cut your holiday short, it's getting serious.

Don't talk about being able to see the sea from your granny's place, I don't want to hear about water, and anyhow I don't believe there's so much water in the world — even if it's salty! It's still stinking hot here. No rain since you left, not a single drop, and the cattle are going to hell in a bucket. Another two bores carked it last week, so the situation's getting really serious. Your dad's very smart to be a pharmacist (say hello from me), it sure beats farming right now, which is for very thin, very poor people who don't pay bills or eat anything except beef, scrawny chooks and eggs. Even our vegie garden and orchard look crook. Send food parcels — especially honey cakes!

You know I told you I was thinking about trying to find Dad's family and I didn't know what I was doing, and kept getting knock-back letters? Well, I've finally taken a great leap — forward, I hope.

This afternoon I met this great woman, Rose Bannock, from the Koori Co-op in the Valley, who's really easy to talk to and reckons she can help. I ended up telling her about me and Sarah and the twins, how Finn and Ang are Chinese cousins, and even about you being Greek. She laughed at that and said it 'sounded a bit like the history of Australia, or how it could have been. How it should have been in a perfect world.'

It's funny — like I told Rose, when we were little, we used to play a game called that — History of Australia. The twins and I were the Aborigines, Finn was the Chinese miner and Sarah and Angie were the white settlers. Sarah and Angie liked it, but the other four of us got jack of it, we always ended up being dead or pulling Sarah and Ang around in the billycart!

(Hard bit coming!) I couldn't get started with telling her what I was doing. Finally, after edging around the subject for ages, (by telling her about that dumb game and about Sarah wanting to learn to track properly and Dad not being able to teach her anything, and a whole lot of stuff like that), well, finally, I told her about the look I saw on Dad's face whenever he was asked about his family. It was awful, I kept crying when I tried to talk about it.

She really understood. She said she'd seen a whole lot of people before me crying about this, particularly in the last few years, and she'd heard a hundred stories like it.

She talked to me for ages about growing up as a Koori in the 1960s, about how heart-breaking things were for Dad's generation. She told me about the awful life that the little kids had at the Whitehills Orphanage, how they were often taken by force from their families. She called it a 'loveless, alien culture'. When she talked about how desperate the families were, I just sat there shocked dumb.

Kes put her pen down and let her thoughts drift out the window, over the black invisible mountains and up amongst the stars.

Before she started this search, Kes hadn't

thought much about her father's early life. She knew
it had been lonely, but now he had Kate and four kids.
If she remembered it at all, she thought that was
enough.

Talking with Rose, she found herself trembling
with rage. It was a new dimension to her world. The
words 'stolen children' suddenly made sense and she
realised with horror that it was her father she'd been
reading about in the papers. Her own father had possibly, no probably, been one of the stolen children.

When Rose spoke, she felt different for the first
time in her life, as if her Aboriginality was enfolding
her as her innocence was flying out the door. As Rose
pointed out, unless her father was an orphan, she and
her brothers and sister had been cut off from their
grandparents and all their relatives on their father's
side. They might have another unknown family.

Kes found it hard to go on writing, but Gill
would be furious with her if she didn't.

Something's changed in me, Gill, after today. I
wish like hell you were here. I'd make you come
and stay and bash your ears all night. At least
doing it this way I suppose you can put it down
when you get sick of reading all this stuff or
when you reckon I've lost it completely.

I think it's got something to do with never
having felt particularly — anything before — I

mean I was just an ordinary kid, like you. We had trouble with a few kids at school — but it was always from those real dickheads, wasn't it, or new kids feeling insecure? We had lots of friends in primary school, and it just went on the same in high school. I never expected anything different. You didn't either, did you? Did you? Tell me truthfully. I never really expected to be treated differently by kids I grew up with.

Kes thought about the fights at school. When she was caught up in them, she sometimes copped abuse because of her colour; Gill copped it because she was Greek. It always died out pretty quickly. There'd be a few days of snapping and snarling, then things would be back to normal again — or else it came from such losers that it didn't worry her for long. It couldn't. She couldn't stay mad with kids like the poor overweight Tuckey kid in her year, whose stupid parents had called him Ken, and who always got heaps.

Kes sighed. She was getting tired.

So I never thought about being Aboriginal very much, I'm just what I am. Now I feel as if I've almost been living a lie, that I should have known things before; but it never felt wrong before, Gill. I wish you were here. I was just one of the mob. Black and white and yellow and brindle, Dad calls us.

Talking with Rose was weird, I began to see myself as looking the same outside but different inside. It was a bit shocking, as if somewhere in there I'd got lost. The real Kes was wandering around loose inside, not fitting any more. I know it's stupid, but that's what it felt like.

I think it's becoming as much a search for me to find my family, as it is to find Dad's — even though they're the same thing. Does that make sense? I've realised we could have aunts, uncles and cousins, a whole second family I'd never dreamed of. Slow, hey? Rose Bannock has promised to dig into the Whitehills records and interstate birth records through an organisation called Link-Up. Anyway, by the end of today I feel battered. Probably like you do, so I'll shut up. It's two in the morning and my eyes are falling out. Everyone else has been asleep for hours.

I can hear a possum scolding in the gums behind the orchard and an old cow's calling up on the ridge. A dog's barking so far away it must be down in Federation. The stars are very bright and beautiful. It's the only time it's cool and if I stretch my imagination, I can make the gums smell damp — just.

I really really wish you were here — did I say that already? Would it help if I lied and said Finn was going out with Shelley Andrews?

Thank you for listening to all this crazy stuff. I miss you heaps. See you in five weeks.

Much love,
Kes

Chapter 8

SARAH WAS DETERMINED to learn to track, and if her father couldn't teach her, she'd teach herself. She borrowed a book on animal signs and tracking from the mobile library and memorised every word and illustration in it.

To the annoyance of everyone in both families, she borrowed all their shoes, and in the old sandpit, taught herself everyone's footprints. Shoes, sandals, thongs, gumboots, all ended up in the yard. More than once her father or her uncle Charlie came outside shouting, 'Sarah, damn it, where the hell are you? Bring me back my boots.'

The twins alone didn't care, they had a ready-made excuse for running around barefoot. 'Sarah's got our runners, Mum, and she's lost them.'

Sarah developed the habit of walking with her eyes fixed on the ground in front of her, tracking the comings and goings of every person in the place.

She also developed the annoying habit of questioning everyone. 'What were you doing down at the dam, Jack? You're not allowed to play with the pump,' or 'Why were you two behind the chook sheds? Smoking, I suppose. Hope it made you sick.' 'Did you find what you were looking for in the garage, Auntie Mai?' and 'Don't swing on the clothes hoist, Jack, you'll bend it,' or 'Who was the strange person, a man I think, who was wearing boots about size ten, who came to visit you today, Mum?'

'God Almighty,' said Mai. 'It's like living with the Spanish Inquisition. I can't walk across the yard without having to account for my time, actions and intentions.'

'Mum, Kes is turning her feet over in her old brown shoes. I think she needs a new pair, it's not good for her ankles,' or 'Why were you wearing your school shoes out in the paddock, Finn? You got them clogged up with something, too, cow shit probably,' and 'Don't think you tricked me, Jon, wearing Dad's boots, you're only half his weight and you leave drag trails behind you — and anyway, you fell over. I found your hand-print.'

After she'd memorised every pair of shoes that everyone on the farm owned she started on the animals; the three cattle dogs, Blue, Red and the pup Ella, the cat and its kittens, Emma, and the horses, Fred and Freda.

By this time even her victims had to admit, grudgingly, that she was good. Her best effort came one evening at the dinner table when she told her father that Freda was lame in her front foot. Pat said that Freda was perfectly all right. Sarah was adamant that she wasn't, said her hoof had a split, and she was limping a little.

Everyone trudged out into the home paddock. Kate caught Freda and inspected her hoof.

'Sarah's right. The hoof is split. Did you look at this, Sarah?'

'No. I told you, you can see it in her tracks. Why would I need to look at it? Look.' She moved the horse away. 'Look, see there, it's plain in the dust. Well, can't you all see it?'

The others shook their heads.

'If you can tell she has a split hoof from that heap of dust, you're pretty good,' said Pat.

'I'm going to finish dinner,' said Kes, 'it'll be stone cold.'

Angie, always loyal, thought she was wonderful. Everyone else thought she was a pain in the neck.

When Sarah had finished with the house yard, she started out on the swamp. Even Kate, usually tolerant of her daughter's enthusiasms, had to admit it was a relief to have her move a bit further away. 'It's like being removed from a list of police suspects,' she said to Kes.

The inseparable threesome of Sarah, Angie and Emma, now old enough to shadow Angie wherever she went, spent days on their hands and knees out on the claypan, identifying the tracks of every bird and beast that travelled across it. Early morning and evening were the best times, when the sun was low and slight shadows made the tracks stand out. They became so skilled that at these times of day they could stand at the edge of the claypan and identify each creature new to the area and every new track made since the night before.

The emus and roos were simple. The girls knew where they fed and slept, whether the animals were feeding quietly on the edges or if something had startled them.

Each night, Sarah had a new piece of information to announce at dinner.

'Snake-Eyes is about to speak,' said Jon. 'Will the family please kneel.'

'Shut up, space-brain!' Sarah kicked him under the table.

'Aaah! She touched me! She touched me! Do it again. Oh, please, Snake-Eyes, touch me!'

Sarah hit him. 'Jealous little freak.'

'Stop it, you two, or leave the table,' said Pat quietly. 'Sarah, leave him alone. It's your turn, you don't have to fight him.'

'There's a dingo moved into the swamp. It's new. And there's a goanna down the end near the soak where there's still a dribble of water.'

'And did a blowie land on the second gum tree from the gate?' asked Jon.

'We found the remains of a small emu, probably one of Emma's brood, a fox got it maybe a week ago.

You can still see the fox tracks, but the body's almost gone.'

A few nights later, Sarah said, 'Dad, the fox is a female, she's had pups. I think I know where the burrow is, do you want me to show you?'

'Yep. Better do something about that lot or they'll be into the chooks. Thanks, Sarah.'

'We found some tiny tracks. We didn't know what they were, but today we found out they were dunnarts. They eat insects and crawlies and beetles, but they spit out the hard parts of the shells. How many different sorts of dunnarts are there, Mum?'

'Snake-Eyes dunnart know,' Jon shouted.

Sarah pestered her sister about the swamp birds. 'How can I find out about what birds live here, Kes? I see their tracks and I don't know what they are, except for the swans and the ibises. They're easy, but all the others are really hard to tell apart. Kes, do your bird books show their feet?'

'We found the rest of Emma's family,' she said one night, 'there are only three of them left. They're the same size as Emma. They were interested in her, but she was scared of them. It was really sad. That's her family but she didn't know it. She didn't know she once belonged to them.'

I know how she feels, thought Kes.

Pat said Sarah would end up being either a tracker or a podiatrist.

Two days before Christmas everything started to happen.

Kes had banned anyone from coming into the living room. She was making T-shirts for everyone and was having her usual battles with her old enemy the overlocker. At this rate they'd be lucky to have their shirts by Easter. When the phone rang beside her, she nearly jumped out of her skin. It was Rose Bannock.

'I've got news for you, Kes,' she said. 'The Whitehills Orphanage records are intact for the period you want. They're accessible to me on your behalf, if you give me authority to do so.'

Kes gasped.

'Are you there?'

'Yes. I'm just a bit shocked, I guess. I didn't expect it to happen so soon. In fact, I didn't expect it to happen at all, after the knock-backs I got.'

'Some people will go out of their way to be helpful. That's what happened this time. And I've done this before, don't forget, for another family.'

'You didn't get that mean woman who told me it was none of my business? The real snaky one?'

'Oh, Kes! Her!' Rose laughed. 'The awful Miss Hatty. Mad Hatty, they call her. She's just a small fish who picked on you because she could. Made her feel good for a whole week, I bet. No, I bypassed her. Because the records are mostly of Aboriginal kids and families, there are Koori people from Link-Up now collecting and working with the information, so it's not impossible any more. Besides, one of the blokes I talked to was from my people.'

'You make it sound easy. I shouldn't have given up.'

'You didn't give up, it's easier when you know the right channels. Now Kes, don't get your hopes up, but I think I have a good solid lead on at least the area your dad came from.'

'Near here?'

'It could hardly be further. It looks as if his family lived up on the Queensland-New South Wales border, getting out into the dry country.'

'Queensland!' Kes gulped. 'So far away! Why ...? How did he end up down in Melbourne?'

'Kids were moved all over the place. Sometimes so their parents couldn't trace them, particularly if there was a history of that in the area. Sometimes it was simply a matter of convenience for the government department, the kids were sent where there was room for them, even across a continent. Perhaps it was a failed adoption attempt.

'I know families in that area would move their kids back and forwards across the border, depending on where the authorities were coming from at the time. They usually didn't cross the border to grab kids. Your dad must have been unlucky.'

'Poor little devils. It was so cruel.'

'Yes, it was.'

Kes was silent.

'Having second thoughts? Most people do. Just remember this could be good news if you want it.'

'No. Well, yes. No, not really. I don't think so, anyway. But what if he wasn't unlucky, Rose? What if he was just unwanted? Given away?'

'Take your time to decide. This isn't a race. It's a pretty big thing for all of you.'

'Yes. But what if he was just left behind or something, for the authorities to find, or neglected …?'

'Think about it. I won't do anything further until I hear from you again. You can ring me any time, you know, and we'll give it another chew over.'

'OK.'

'If it helps, Kes, I think you're doing the right thing, but that's just me. By far the majority of parents didn't give their kids up; they were stolen. But I'm not in your shoes, or your family's. You have to weigh all that up. I know it was hard on you that day we talked at school, but I was impressed with how you handled it, shock after shock. Did you feel all right after?'

'I spat the dummy with Finn on the way home and haven't felt the same since. If that's OK, then I'm OK. Most of the time.'

Rose laughed. 'You poor old thing. It happens to all of us at some time. Eventually we all have to work out where we sit. Sometimes for kids that grow up in a racist community like I did, it's a fact of life from your earliest memories. You start dealing with it as a tiny kid and you live with it. In some ways you've had it easy, so it's hit you later. There's no hurry for all of this. It's not urgent. Don't rush it or force it. You've got your whole life to puzzle it out.'

'Did you feel split down the middle, caught in a revolving door?'

'Yup. Exactly that, but you've got great insight, Kes. You'll make it. Talk to Finn, he sounds like a pretty cool kind of fella. He might even have a new perspective on it, having a Chinese mother.'

Kes laughed, remembering the bus trip home. 'Yeah, he's OK. For a boy.'

'Kes, I'll leave it up to you to contact me. You'll need to write a letter of authorisation, anyhow, for me to act on your behalf. Tell me exactly how far you want to go. We can stop any time. Have a happy Christmas, Kes.'

'Happy Christmas, Rose, and thanks. Thanks heaps.'

Around lunchtime, the first chicks broke their shells and all afternoon there was a steady hatching. Within hours, they were dry balls of yellow fluff, scratching after food.

'Just stay out of sight, and don't cluck,' Kes warned Finn, 'or you can do an Angie and have a hundred chickens following you around night and day. Do you really want them all roosting on your bed-ends and your bookshelves?'

'I might like a live chicken doona.'

The hatching was very successful. By the next day, from one hundred eggs, they had ninety-four live chickens. All the eggs that were going to had hatched.

The following day, Christmas Eve, Kes made a few ineffective starts at talking to Finn as they cleaned up the incubator. She didn't know where to begin, felt like an idiot, and didn't know if Finn would approve anyway. He could be a real stickler for things he thought might be unfair or 'unethical'. Recently, he'd been talking about 'ethics' at every opportunity. Kes thought that if he told her she was acting unethically, she'd crumble. She was exasperated with herself. She'd never had any trouble talking to him before, and now, when she needed him most, she couldn't even start.

As they were finishing in the hatching shed, clouds started to build up in the western sky. Immense, anvil-shaped thunderheads, that streamed tails out behind them, rose over the hills to the west of Federation, growing taller and blacker as they watched. It was strange, almost unreal, after months of blasting sun. A wind sprang up bringing faint waves of wet-smelling air.

By four o'clock, the clouds had closed in over their heads. The sun went out and the sky turned blue-black. It looked as if they'd get a drenching, torrential rain which, even if most of it ran off the parched paddocks, would put water into the dams and tanks.

Sheet lightning lit up the monstrous clouds from

inside, like great vaulted buildings where some super-human being was throwing the light switches on and off. Echoes of the thunder rolled around the valley and bounced off the mountains. Kes could smell the rain strongly, but still nothing happened.

Like the cattle, the twins got rattier and rattier as the storm built up. Finn was sent out to round up the kids and bring them all inside.

Everyone was in the big wood-panelled dining room of the Lawsons' place when the lightning started forking down on the farm, but still not a drop of rain. Not a single drop. Kes felt as if the sky was pushing her into the ground.

Suddenly, with an incredible deafening explosion, louder than any sound she'd ever experienced, so loud that Kes could feel it through her body, lightning struck a 20-metre pine tree close to the house and blew it apart.

The trunk exploded and, like knives, slivers of wood drove themselves into the ground. Branches shattered and the debris, flung high, landed on shed and garage roofs and rained down on the house. A chunk of wood crashed through Angie's bedroom window.

The twins were trying hard to slide out the door so they could see the action from the verandas. Sarah had her arm around Angie and, together with Emma, they were all squashed into one of the wide old arm-chairs. Every time the thunder crashed, Angie buried her face in Emma's downy feathers.

Through the window, Kes watched the lashing that the property was taking. The wild windstorm had suddenly risen to gale force, as if a cyclone was passing over them.

The trees in the windbreaks close to the house were bent almost double under the assault, branches breaking and flying as they watched.

The cattle turned their backs to the wind or raced, terrified, before it, and, at each thunderclap, they charged to another corner of the paddock.

The three heelers had disappeared under the house at the first sound of thunder. Kes could hear Blue whimpering under the floorboards. Red was growling in a continuous roll under the bathroom and Ella yelped every time there was a crash.

As Kes watched, a sheet of corrugated iron stripped off the hayshed roof, flew like cardboard across the paddock and crashed down amongst the cattle. The poor beasts bolted, panic-stricken.

The violence of the storm lasted twenty minutes and when the lightning and wind stopped as suddenly as they had started, the first drops of rain fell. Everyone ran outside in anticipation, staring at the clouds, willing them to open up and send down a deluge, a great soaking downpour that would wash the air clean. Cool wet air; Kes had forgotten what it tasted like.

Huge drops spat up the dust in the yard, but it came to nothing. The drops didn't even join up, and as soon as it had started, the rain stopped again.

The families watched in despair as a wide arc of sunshine rose on the western horizon and the black ceiling moved past them to the east like a great roof opening.

Charlie, disgusted, wiped a streak of wet dust across his eyes. 'All that sound and fury, as well as that poor old tree going, and not a bloody useful drop of rain to show for it.'

It looked as if a bomb had hit the yard and orchard. The shattered pine tree had exploded into a thousand pieces. Some complete branches hung in strange places, on the clothes line or shrouding the roof of the outside toilet, but most of the tree was shredded into chunks of wood, bark and needles, and flung over every square metre of yard. The post and rail fence of the horse yards between the houses looked like a hedge.

One huge branch had planted itself in the orchard. 'Glad I wasn't under it when that decided to be an apple tree,' said Kate, looking in misery at the immature fruit stripped from the fruit trees. 'All that's left of this year's wretched crop is lying here on the ground.'

The cars and trucks, with a few extra dents, were covered with debris; the greenhouse, a shattered mess of frame, glass and plastic sheeting, was lying on its side in the vegie garden. The old Victorian bird aviary and fernery, which the first Lawsons had built, was wrecked, flattened by the felled tree trunk that had dropped straight across it. Ella was playing with the little gold crown which once had sat on top.

Apart from Angie's broken window and a corner of a veranda on the Martins' house, now a bit wonky, the houses had escaped damage, but it took hours to clean up the yards. The rest could wait until after Christmas Day.

The sky cleared to the eastern horizon and the heat started building again. The cattle were twitchy, startling at the slightest disturbance. They roamed in small restless groups, tossing their heads and head-butting each other.

Kes felt so edgy she could've kicked someone.

Chapter 9

No one slept much that Christmas Eve night. The storm followed by the lack of rain left everyone bad-tempered, except for the twins, who were leaping out of their skins with excitement at the thought of presents. The heat, after the storm front passed, continued to scorch until sundown, when the mercury dropped slowly but never to much below thirty degrees.

Kes was glad to go to bed. The constant racket of the twins was annoying her. She felt too old to be excited like them, and too young to be cranky at them.

She woke after a dream in which she'd battled a faceless thing that held the twins hostage in the centre of a maze of frightening dark passages. The bottom sheet was soaked in sweat.

It was half-past four on Christmas Day, not long after dawn. The twins were already up looking for their presents. Kes could hear them falling over furniture in the living room, whispering and rustling paper. She heard the back door fly open and then bang shut, the dogs bounding after them, Ella barking like an idiot, as they tore across the yard to the old dairy, then their yells as they discovered their new bikes.

Everyone else in the place was awake shortly after, because the twins rode into all their bedrooms, showing off their bikes. Both houses were thoroughly up by five o'clock.

By six o'clock the two families had gathered for Christmas breakfast at the Lawsons' house. Kes had finally finished the T-shirts. They looked good, she thought, except for Charlie's, which got stuck around his ears and her mother's, which somehow had an armhole sewn up.

Finn and Angie gave Kes two of the most beautiful presents she'd ever received. Angie had carved a small red gum pendant for her, Sarah and Finn, and had strung them on fine leather thongs. She'd sanded and polished the wood until it glowed. For Kes, she'd carved a kestrel hovering, for Finn, a dolphin, and for Sarah, a striped emu chick.

Finn had taken an old fence post, grey on the outside, blood red inside, split it, and made small, brass-hinged boxes for everyone. Like the pendants, the interior of the boxes shone deep crimson. Kes was holding hers when the phone rang.

For years after she recalled that moment as a snapshot; the sunny room, the puppy with tinsel around her collar, her mother holding a deep blue bowl and looking out the window, the smell of the card-amom bread fresh from the oven. Finn hugging Angie, her father and Jack laughing at Mai struggling into her T-shirt, slightly on the tight side, Jon firing cherry pips at the dogs, and Finn just turning to speak to her.

Alex McLaren owned the adjoining property, ten kilometres to the north. The far end of his property was on fire, undoubtedly a lightning strike from the night before. The north wind, blowing strongly, was spearheading the fire towards his house — and towards the Lawson and Martin property.

Pat ran out onto the north veranda. Two hours after dawn and it was already stinking hot. The wind blasted dust streamers across the paddocks. A brown cloud of smoke was building to the north, just over the first line of hills. It looked like an atomic cloud rising over the horizon, and just as menacing. Pat could already smell burning. Ten kilometres with a wind blowing, it was no distance! There was truly no time.

He ran back inside. Mai was still on the phone to Alex McLaren, talking rapidly, arranging to help evacu-ate the McLaren children and notify the fire fighting crews in Federation.

For a moment frozen in time, Kes held Angie's pendant against her neck and stared at the great spiral of brown smoke growing behind the hills. Like the storm last night, which had ignited this fire, another catastrophe was coming at them out of a clear blue sky.

No kid grew up in this region without knowing

exactly what to do in case of bushfire. Finn and Angie ran to their rooms and Kes raced Sarah and the twins back to their house. They had to pack a bag, one bag only of essential things, dress in woollen clothes, horrible in the heat, put on boots, not shoes, and get back to the other house in less than three minutes.

Kes was shaking. All the times she'd cursed those fire practices! Once, their parents had even dragged them all out of bed in the middle of the night! Now, her mind kept racing from one instruction to another; stay in the house unless you are absolutely certain it's safe to get away in the car or the truck; don't forget the woollen blankets, they have to be woollen, wool doesn't burn or melt onto your skin. If you're caught in the car, stay there until the fire front passes; the initial heat from the fire will kill you, protect yourself from the fire front; get under the blanket, stay low, crawl, avoid the smoke.

She could hear her parents' voices over and over in her head. 'Above all, stay calm, Kes, you can't think if you panic; the younger ones will follow you.' She hoped they couldn't see how close she was to it, as she packed and dressed them. She tried to encourage them with a smile that felt pasted onto her face.

Kes threw her own clothes on, pushing her head through a horrible old brown woollen jumper that smelt of dirty runners. She hurried Sarah and the twins back to the Lawsons' house. As she reached the veranda, she looked back at her own home through the orchard. It already looked abandoned, left to its fate. She wondered if she'd see it at the end of the day, ever sleep in her bedroom again, or would it be just smoking ruins of black stumps and twisted roofing iron, like those awful pictures on TV? She couldn't even think for a moment what she'd miss most if the whole place did burn, then she remembered the small brown photograph of her father, and for a split second hesitated, wanting desperately to go back again. She stopped in the yard, turned, but Mai yelled at her, and she knew she'd run out of time.

Mai had the van out of the garage. Sarah and the twins were scrambling in. Angie was screaming at Mai, refusing to get into the car unless Emma was allowed to come too. Mai shouted at Angie to do as she was told. Angie shouted back that Emma was not going to lose her mother again. Emma, terrified by the yelling, jumped in through the open door. Angie leapt in after her and locked the door, scowling at Mai through the window. Emma was coming.

Kate was planning to stay, to put out spot fires and mop up if the front came close to them. Kes and Finn asked to stay with her. Pat looked at them for a long moment, trying to weigh up the risk against the help they could be if it came to saving the houses.

'Let them stay,' said Charlie, scanning the northern sky, watching the twisting smoke cloud. 'Kate can't stay here alone, either. That front is heading out to the south-west, I reckon, I doubt it'll travel back this way.

The fire bunker will protect them, if the worst comes to the worst. Let them stay, they're old enough.'

'They'll be a lot older after this is over,' said Kate.

Mai left. She had to pick up the McLaren children along the road and get back off the track before the fire came through. They just had time to make it safely to Federation, if nothing went wrong and Ellen McLaren got her children to the pick-up point in time.

As Mai left, they could hear the first of the fire trucks coming down the road. They passed the Lawson turn off and continued on to McLarens'. Charlie and Pat threw the motorbikes onto the farm truck and left to join the fire-fighters on the front blazing in the forested ranges between the McLarens' and their property.

The three left at the house frantically made preparations. Kate opened the fire bunker dug into a bank of earth near the dam. It smelt stale and it sounded as if rats were living inside. She caught the dogs, already trembling with fear, and shut them in it.

On the roof of the Martins' house, Kes and Finn flung off the debris that still covered it after yesterday's storm. They worked swiftly; raking and throwing the volatile pine needles and gum leaves away from the house. Finally, when the roof was clear, they blocked the downpipes with the big rubber plugs that hung on chains off the spouting. Kate started the pump from the dam and flooded the gutters of both houses.

The blue sky shrank rapidly under an immense, expanding pall of smoke, until the whole sky was obscured in choking brown clouds. Suffocating waves of it rolled down from the hills and enveloped them. At times it became impossible to see through the smoke, a terrifying fog in which they worked blind, with no knowledge of where the fire was travelling. Occasionally patches cleared and they could tear the scarves off their faces and breathe blessed clear air for a moment. In one break, through streaming eyes, they saw the fire racing along the back of the ranges beyond the waterhole, its leading edge travelling wickedly fast.

Kate saturated the hessian bags, filled every trough, bucket and container she could find with water and hosed down the vine-covered trellises, cursing the dead leaves caught in the branches. They were like shredded paper waiting for a spark to drop.

Kes and Finn raced through the houses, closing windows and doors behind them. Kes hesitated in her own bedroom, then tipped out her storage box, grabbed the old photo of her father and shoved it into an inside pocket. In her parents' bedroom, she found her mother's rings lying on top of her chest of drawers and slipped them on. She looked around urgently. What else should she take? It was too hard. She grabbed an unframed photo of her father and mother she knew her mum loved.

Kes raced down the passage into the twins' room, slammed their windows and door and finally,

choking on the smoke, ran around the veranda checking outside doors.

Kate had started the sprinklers hooked to the
dam pump. Fountains of water sprang up on what had
once been deep green lawns surrounding the houses.

Fred and Freda were in the house yard. Kate
captured the frightened and resisting old horses,
coaxed them into the stone milking shed and barred
the door against their wild kicks and plunges. The
smoke had brought them close to panic. The cats had
already disappeared under the house and would have
to take their chances.

Kes met the other two in the yard. Finn had just
finished in the Lawson house and was hauling a yellow
fire hose from under the house as Kate attached the
other end to their biggest water tank.

Above them, the sun shone as a brilliant copper
disk through reddish smoke, a halo of rainbow colours
encircled it, with a luminous false sun reflected on
either side. If it weren't such a hideous sight, it'd be
beautiful, Kes thought.

To the north, the smoke cleared again as the
wind swung around, blowing the fire to the west. They
could see that the front had leapt onto the back of the
ridge that encircled the swamp, waterhole and home
paddocks. The flames were burning deep into the
valleys and racing up the back slope to its crest.

'Jesus Christ,' breathed Kate, 'It's not much more
than two ks away.'

The fire was burning faster and stronger than they had feared or expected, outlining trees on the ridge top for brief seconds before they exploded in great fountains of showering sparks.

Suddenly, the flames topped the ridge, not in a single place as they had anticipated, but in a 10-kilometre-long wall of fire. Then they could hear it roaring, like an approaching train.

'If it keeps going across the ridge in that direction with the wind behind it, I think we'll be OK here. It might just miss the houses,' said Kate. 'Look, there it goes!'

The front suddenly broke away from the ridge top, carrying everything before it in a terrifying swoop over the crest, rolling down into the gully and out onto the home paddocks. The low trees exploded before the fire touched them. Waves of flames rippled across the dry grass and leapt into the stands of shade timber. Huge trees ignited in a second as the fire crowned, jumping from clump to clump. Once, Finn caught sight of a mob of cattle stampeding before the flames. He turned away, sick. He couldn't bear to watch.

As the fire raged along the ridge, hot ash and smouldering leaves began cascading down. Burning cinders fell on their hats and blew around the yard. A large ember stuck and burnt a hole in Finn's jumper. They soaked each other with the hoses and worked rapidly, dousing the burning debris that fell faster and thicker about them. A small branch, still flaming, fell on Kes's arm. Fear jerked her arm away, she'd nearly screamed. Her whole world was burning up over the top of them. Spot fires were starting in the yard. A small flicker of flame ran up through the shrubs beside the garage, another was starting in dried leaves behind the dairy. As she watched, a burning branch dropped onto the flattened glasshouse and caught the torn plastic sheeting.

A blast of intense heat caught them. With sudden horror, Kate realised that the front had changed. A shift in the wind was blasting it right back into their faces. The fire that had been racing away from them a minute ago, now surged back across the home paddock, building into a wall of flame coming directly at them.

'That's it,' yelled Kate across the yard. 'We can't do any more. Into the bunker. Come on. Run!'

Flames flowed along the windbreaks, splitting into two, three, then four arms that would converge again on the houses. The pine trees went up like fireworks, but the eucalypts, exploding before the flames reached them, erupted from within and flung burning branches out into the dry grass.

'Come on, Kes! Move it.' Kate raced towards her. 'Kes! Move it. Finn, for Christ's sake, grab her! Kes! **Kes!!**'

They had only minutes before the fire would envelop them. Kes turned and tried to make herself run. Finn's shimmering face appeared close to hers, his mouth open. He must be shouting, she thought. I wonder why he moves so slowly when the fire's coming.

An inferno of flames, thirty, perhaps forty metres high was rolling down on them, carrying everything before it. Finn grabbed for her. She seemed to have no substance as her hand slipped through his. He grabbed her again, screaming, 'Kes! Come on! Kes!', knowing he had to hold her until she was safe or lose her.

It seemed to Kes as if she and Finn were being blown like leaves in yesterday's gale and, holding hands as they had when they were children, were floated down the slope towards the dam. She had no sensation of her feet touching the ground, she was only conscious of a towering wall of flame at her back, propelling her forward on its bow wave. Like a fiery dolphin, she was surfing the burning air.

The first blast of scorching air hit them as they fell into the doorway of the bunker.

They slammed the door shut. It was pitch-black and suddenly blessedly cool.

Kate guided Kes to a seat and sat beside her, holding her.

Finn felt over the wall for the lanterns. His hand was shaking so badly that the match kept going out. It seemed the ultimate irony — his world was on fire — and five metres away from it he couldn't light a match. Kate took the matches, lit the lantern, then with an arm around each of them, sat and waited.

The heelers, cowering under the bench seats, came out slowly to be calmed. Finn picked up little Ella, and Blue and Red crowded their legs.

Outside, the world was going mad. Through the thick metal door they could hear the holocaust overtake them and roar past. They dared not open the door, the air would be too hot to breathe and they'd catch the full blast of it.

They waited and waited.

Kes' hand went to her neck. 'I've lost Angie's carving.' They were the first words she had spoken since that strange flight down the hill.

Kate hugged her tighter. 'I'm sure she'll carve you another one.'

'No! I want that one.' Its loss made Kes feel desolate, as if the last of her luck had flown and she was unprotected. Superstition, she told herself — there's no place for self-indulgence here — but it didn't help much.

Two thunderous booms reverberated in the dugout as something huge exploded. Kes felt it through her body.

'I hope that was petrol containers in the shed and not the gas tanks behind the house,' said Kate.

'Do you think the houses are still standing?' Finn's voice didn't sound like his own.

'Don't know, Finn. We did everything we could. As it was, it was a close call. If that's the gas tanks, nothing'll be standing. If the houses have blown apart or burnt, they've gone. We're safe. We have to believe that the others are safe, too, and that's all that matters.'

'Right.' Kes was hoping she sounded confident. She stared at her hands.

'I got your rings, Mum,' she said, slipping them off, 'and some photos.' Kes took the photos out of her pocket, acutely aware that if the gas tanks had blown, these were all that remained of their home.

Kate's eyes filled with tears. 'Thank you, my darling Kes.' She held her daughter's shuddering body close to her.

They waited. And waited more. After the longest twenty minutes of their lives, and when the worst of the noise had died down, they cautiously opened the door.

It was like looking through a crack into the gates of hell.

The fire front was receding now in a towering wall of flame tearing apart the bush on the far side of the road, rolling away towards the edge of the plateau before it dropped down onto Federation.

They stood sheltering from the heat in the doorway. The immediate and most obvious thing was that both houses were still standing. The garage was on fire and, as they watched, the petrol tank of Kes' old red truck blew, blasting the garage roof open like a silver flower, exploding sheets of galvanised iron and shards of metal all over the yard.

The garden shed, blown apart by the exploding petrol cans, was burning fiercely. The bank of fire protection trees planted closest to the house was blackened and shrivelled, but the trees hadn't caught.

Kate cautiously stepped outside. The heat on her face and feet was incredible but bearable, as if the air she was breathing and the ground itself was burning under the soles of her boots.

'OK. It's sort of safe.' Kate didn't sound too sure. 'That is, if nothing else explodes. Unless the houses catch, or the flames reach the ute or the tractor, I don't think there's anything much left to blow up.'

The houses, the stone milking shed and the corrugated-iron chook sheds running down the slope from the devastated orchard, appeared to be the only buildings still standing.

The garage, haysheds, garden shed, outside toilet and the old washhouse were all burning fiercely. Spot fires were burning all around the yard. Every garden bed, even the vegie garden and the orchard, was alight. The stockyard, worksheds and wooden fences were blazing. Everything that could burn was in flames. Except for the houses. It was a miracle.

'Fred and Freda have survived,' said Kes. The frantic animals were kicking the dairy apart.

'What the storm and fire didn't bring down, the horses will,' said Kate. 'They'll have to stay there. They'll charge off in a panic and kill themselves if I let them out.

'I think we'd better see if we can take this heat and get up to the houses. There's a fire near Sarah's room I can see from here. Another next to the side door. We don't know what's happening round the back.'

'The ute and the tractor are around there,' said Finn. 'Least I hope they still are.'

'OK, now listen — don't put yourself in danger — watch for things falling. Kes, you and I'll work together at the houses. Are you all right, Kes?' Kes nodded. 'The backpacks of water are by the front doors; we'll get them on first. Finn, can you try to get that bloody pump at the dam going again? It looks from here as if the fire has missed it, but it's stopped, it'll be the heat. Don't anyone forget, there's probably no electricity, that'll be gone, but don't touch anything or get water on any wires. I might be wrong.'

The backpacks, full of water, were incredibly heavy, but even so, they seemed to run out distressingly fast. Fires were burning on the verandas of both houses, the dry leaves fuelling the flames that ran through the grapevines.

Kes and Kate seemed to be battling against impossible odds. As they doused one spot, another would leap into flames nearby. Kes pumped water onto a fire that had taken hold under the eaves and was threatening to catch the wall of her room. Small fires burnt on the roofs, one had started under the steps of the Lawsons' house and was licking up the edge of the veranda. The old stuffed couch on the front steps was well alight by the time Kate reached it. Angie's broken window had allowed a fire to start in her bedroom. Kate felt sick when she found it. It had burnt a big hole in the quilt on Angie's bed and was still smouldering.

Against the bargeboards beneath the twins' room, a mass of windblown debris had collected. The base of the wall on the back of the Martins' house was burning fiercely, threatening to catch the whole house. Kate attacked the fire with the fire hose she'd attached to the water tank. The pressure wasn't great, the electric pressure pump was out, but the hose reached and the stream of water allowed her to flood the wall.

Kes was onto her third refill of water when they heard Finn's triumphant shout from the dam, and the petrol pump that ran the garden hoses kicked into life again.

Spouts of water sprang up all around the houses again. It was like a breath from heaven. For a long blissful moment, Kes drenched herself under the spray. The water steamed off her clothes.

Finn came running up from the dam, jubilant, dragging a very long hose that had survived, and attached it to the most central tap in the yard. A strong jet of water shot out, quenching the flames that were still leaping up out of nowhere, seemingly intent on finally getting a hold on the Lawsons' house. Great clouds of steam rose from the walls and roofs as he hosed down the weatherboards and iron roofing.

Some of the walls of the Martins' house were so hot that they were smouldering, a degree or two away from bursting into flames. One wall that Finn hosed crumbled into a heap of charcoal. The water shot through it straight inside.

'Hey! Watch it!' shouted Kate, 'That's my kitchen you're messing up there. I left the Christmas cake on the table!' Through the wall, Finn glimpsed it skid across the kitchen table and disappear off the edge.

The water sprinklers were starting to cool the surrounds of the houses. At least it was now possible to work near them without roasting from the reflected heat off the walls or finding you were standing in burning leaves.

Kes attached the three remaining hoses to functioning taps. All the external walls of the houses were now within reach, and barring something unforeseen, with the walls and roofs wet, the houses would be safe if they could keep the burning leaves, still swirling down from the trees, from getting a hold on the roofs.

Kes kept circling the houses, checking the verandas and eaves. She couldn't believe that water could dry so quickly or that wicked tongues of flames could appear from thin air every time she turned her back, starting spot fires in places she'd just hosed down.

The garage and sheds were hissing piles of black, smoking mess. The wooden fences, as far as they could see through the smoke, were all burning, as was every tree in the home paddock. The big old trees kept crashing down, those close to the houses sending up clouds of burning debris that drifted down and covered them in smouldering leaves, but the paddocks themselves were now bare, black and smoking. The grass that had managed to hold on through the drought had burnt, and the flaming debris blown from the trees could do no further damage.

Apart from the long, once dense windbreaks planted along every fence that were still burning fiercely, there was nothing left to destroy.

They were drenching the surrounds of the house and the smouldering flattened wreckage of the buildings in the yard, when they heard the first of the fire trucks belting down the road from the McLarens'.

'Poor devils, they must be frantic about us,' said Kate, waving her hat. 'They had no way of telling where that front went when it topped the hill and swung back around onto us. They'll have no idea if we even survived. Or if anything's left standing.'

The fire truck came tearing up the track. As it swung into the yard, Pat and Charlie leapt off the back.

'My God, you're safe,' cried Pat, choking with tears, gathering Kate and Kes into his arms. Charlie picked up Finn as if he were three years old, carried him to the charred veranda steps and sat cradling him.

'We got cut off,' said Pat. 'The road out of McLarens' was cut when the front swung around. We knew it was heading here. There wasn't a bloody thing we could do. We were on our way back, but we got trapped in there.' Pat buried his face in Kate's neck. 'I thought you'd be caught by the front. I thought you'd all be killed and I'd let you stay.'

'It's OK, Dad. We're all safe.' Kes patted his back. 'We got into the dugout well before the front arrived. We didn't take chances.'

'Where are Mai and the kids?' Kate asked. She'd started to shake and had to sit down.

'Down in Federation. The fire's bypassed the town. We know they're safe, we got onto them by radio. Everyone this side of the mountain is down there by now. Except the fire crews and you three. You're the only ones cut off. Everyone's worried sick about you. I never should've let you stay. The houses could've burnt to the ground for all I care.'

'But they haven't, Dad, we saved them. They're OK. We're OK. Stop shaking. We're all safe.' Kes held her father very tightly. It was a long time before he calmed down enough to try to grin at her.

'The main road and the back track down into the valley stayed open when the front changed direction,' said Pat. The Bellesinis, near neighbours on the far side of the range, were already in Federation when the fire came through. They were on their way to Melbourne to spend Christmas with Maria's parents. 'They've lost everything, house, stock, sheds — the lot. They've been hit for six. They've only got what they stand up in. The O'Connells have lost their house, too, the fire dropped off the ridge behind them and swept up everything in its path. They didn't have a chance, they only just got themselves out in the nick of time.'

'The McLarens' house is OK,' Charlie added, 'but their paddocks are destroyed and they'll have lost a lot of stock, I'd say. Every other family, the Carters, the Andrews and the Taylors, were able to get out. Old Mr and Mrs Nicholson are safe, the police evacuated them. They all had more warning than we did, a few precious extra minutes. Their stock will have been wiped out, like ours, but they're all safe. Even if the fire swings back through the town now, everyone there can get shelter in the Federation mine tunnel. That's big enough to take the entire population and a few thousand extra.'

The crew of the fire truck rolled out the hoses and saturated the houses, the smouldering remains of the sheds, the garage and what had once been cattle yards. The horses were led out of the milking shed, wild-eyed and jumpy.

Finn said, 'But the houses survived. We got it right, didn't we, Dad?'

'Quite honestly, right now I don't care if the houses are standing or not,' said Charlie, 'I just wanted to see you three standing there safe. Ask me in an hour if I'm glad about the houses.'

'But yes, Finn,' added Pat, 'you all got it right, all right. Very, very right.'

All five of them were black, streaked with grime and water. Their charred clothes were dripping, their eyes, swollen with smoke, showed bloodshot in their filthy faces, and they stank.

A second fire truck arrived. One of the fire crew suggested that the five of them take the ute and join the rest of the family in Federation. The radio operator said he'd called down and their families in town knew that everyone was safe, but Mai told him, very loudly, that they actually wanted them there, to see and touch.

It was then that Kes remembered that it was still Christmas Day. It was lunchtime; they should all be sitting down to turkey, ham and Christmas pudding. 'Funny,' she said, 'the turkey's the only thing around here that isn't cooked.'

'Well, perhaps we should've thrown it out the window when we saw the front coming,' said Kate. 'Come on. Let's go. I need a break from this for an hour or so.'

Chapter 10

ON BOXING DAY, Finn sat on the charred stump of a burnt-out fence post looking at the row of silent chook sheds. He was thinking about a picture book that he'd loved when he was a little kid. He still had it somewhere in his room. It started, 'My name is Ajani. I live in Africa. Although my land is very poor, I will not leave my home.' The first page of that book had been going around in his brain all day. 'My name is Finn. I live in the Baw Baws. Although my land is very burnt, I will not leave my home.'

Yesterday, when the fire reached the sheds, with the radiant heat and the scorching north wind blowing smoke straight into them, the chooks had suffocated. Thousands of them died.

Of all the white leghorn layers, only about twenty sick-looking birds survived; of the table hens and the newly hatched chickens, none.

It was the silence that was so eerie; the chooks dead, the cattle dead, no birds calling. The farm was silent, humans the only living things still moving about.

Finn's world was reduced to disgusting black wreckage. Horribly blackened and misshapen cattle carcasses lay in the paddock corners, their bodies charred, their eye sockets still staring in terror. It was like some gruesome barbecue. Finn could smell burnt flesh over the pervading smell of burnt vegetation. It made him retch. He'd never eat meat again. Ever.

The ranges were black and smoking; the paddocks black and bare; the trees, black stumps; the yard, black and stinking.

Finn had no idea how they'd make it through the next few days, let alone the coming year. It had been bad enough before. The drought had stretched them to breaking point — he was pretty sure this would snap them. Probably all the remaining cattle, certainly the best of the breeding stock, had died in the fire. Thirty selected breeders, on supplementary feed in the home paddock, had all died. The rest had been running in the ranges paddocks, the area that suffered the worst damage.

No one had been out there yet, but that would be the next job. Pat and Charlie would go out with guns and shoot the injured beasts, if any had survived. Finn doubted it.

He kicked the side of the shed and the burnt iron caved in under his foot. Through the gaping hole were more chook carcasses. He swore. There was no way they could hang onto the farm. His greatest fear was that they'd be forced out and have to live in a city in the

Latrobe Valley, or worse, in Melbourne itself. He couldn't imagine being cooped up in a suburban block with neighbours all around him and traffic on his doorstep. He'd suffocate in the Valley, he couldn't breathe down there. It'd be like living a nightmare, like the nights he woke up with his face in the pillow, dreaming he was drowning.

He kicked the shed again, wiping away the tears of anger.

Kes and Sarah had been gone for hours. It was as if everyone was lost today. There was a heap of work to do and no one had the heart to start. The twins had taken off. Their bikes survived only because they had them parked in their bedroom. The burnt hills were so denuded of vegetation that every now and then Finn could see them crossing the grey face of the slopes where yesterday there had been dense under-growth in a hundred shades of green and brown. Their new tyres would be wrecked riding over that smoking hillside, Finn thought absently. He didn't care. It didn't matter.

He watched Pat and Kate standing by the remains of the cattle-loading ramp. His parents came out and joined them. They just stood there, as if they were in shock, scuffing the ground and staring at the black hills.

Mai said something and Charlie threw down his coffee cup and stalked away. Pat said something to Kate and she snapped at him.

Angie, watching them from a distance, turned away and crept up beside him. He moved over to make room for her and tried to smile. 'Crook, eh, little sis?'

'Finn, what's going to happen to us? Mum just said to Dad that we're so broke now that it wouldn't matter if any of the cattle survived; we'll only be eating them. Then Pat said that if the houses had burnt at least we'd have some insurance to live on. Kate said, thanks a lot, next time she'd remember that and let everything burn. They don't mean it, do they?'

Finn put his arm around her. 'Ang, everyone's so upset, don't take any notice of *anything* anyone says for at least three days. Promise me. Everyone's talking crazy. And I'll tell you this — the only way we'll leave here is starving and naked, and we're a long way from that.'

'What'll Mum and Dad do?'

'Dunno. They'll have to make some nasty decisions. We all will. I can't leave school at fifteen; I'm too young. So's Kes.'

'You aren't allowed to leave school!' Angie searched his face. 'You're going to be a vet, like me.'

'You can forget about that,' he said, the anger welling again. 'There won't even be enough money to finish school, so forget about uni.'

Angie's eyes filled with tears. 'It won't always be this bad.'

'No, it'll get worse. If we have to leave here, it

will. Oh, geez. I'm sorry, Angie.' Finn hugged her. 'We're not leaving. We're not. OK? Come on. I can't stand this sitting around. It's really getting to me. I've got to do something. I'm going to start cleaning up something. Come and help me, will you? I've got to get my mind off this, I can't face the chooks yet.'

'Don't leave school, please, Finn,' Angie pleaded, catching him.

Finn shook his head. 'I can't. Yet. It's illegal, so that's that. We'll have to think up another scheme. I suppose we could try the chooks again, but it makes me feel sick even looking at them.'

Kate thought it'd be a good idea if they could still try to have a late Christmas dinner. It was the worst idea anyone had had for quite a while.

There was no power and no one felt like firing up the wood stove. Mai said that she'd had enough fire to last her a lifetime. Just the thought of lighting it and seeing the flames catch made Finn feel shaky. They'd eat cold what was already cooked.

The twins had been in big trouble for riding their bikes on the slopes near trees that were still burning. They were very subdued.

Sarah's arm was bandaged from a burn she'd got in the wreckage of the hayshed. Kes had burnt a hole in the bottom of her new jeans and had a deep, jagged gash on her ankle. They'd all been banned from leaving the yard until the fire crews had mopped up the last of the fires on the slopes.

They salvaged what was left of Christmas dinner. The uncooked turkey, with no refrigeration, was turning bad in the heat. The cooked ham was still edible, but the Christmas cake that Finn had washed off the table when he blasted a hole in the smouldering kitchen wall, was a write-off. They found it lying beside the fridge, a waterlogged mess.

The Christmas pudding, stored in a slatted cupboard, which had also been in the firing line of Finn's hose, was edible — just. It wasn't bad cold and the melted ice cream was an OK sauce under the circumstances.

Kes couldn't stop her mind going back to the garage blowing up and how her lovely old red truck splattered all over the yard. She heard the explosion over and over in her head. Every time she thought of it, her eyes would fill with tears and she'd have to look away. It was such a stupid thing to think about when they could've been hurt or killed. Or lost the houses. When the cattle were dead. But it wouldn't stop; the harder she tried, the more often she heard it. The soft thump, then the massive explosion, then the roof opening up like a pair of hands and the red roof of the cab flying out.

The others seemed to be doing the same thing. Every few minutes someone's mind would wander off and they'd get a far-away look in their eyes. Finn started to say something about clearing out the chook sheds and had to stop.

The worst thing was the stench that pervaded everything. It was worse outside, but even the food they ate smelled burnt, making Kes gag. It was stupid to try, as if they were pretending things were normal when they all knew they were in a disaster zone.

Finn pushed his plate away. Eating reminded him of dead chooks and the blackened carcasses in the paddocks.

Angie was surreptitiously feeding her ham to Emma under the table.

Kes walked out onto the veranda. She'd never felt so hopeless.

From inside Kate screamed in rage, 'My beautiful Christmas pudding! That bloody emu's eating it!' She threw a pan at Emma who squawked in fear and bolted out the door.

'Don't hurt Emma!' yelled Angie, running out to her rescue. 'You're so cruel!'

'Emma! Angie! Angie!' Kate called after her, 'I'm sorry. Oh, hell!'

Pat came out and sat on the steps, his head in his hands.

Kes sat down silently beside him, her arms around him. It was no use saying everything was going to be OK. It was as clear as day that it wasn't. She traced the birthmark on the back of his elbow with her finger. It had fascinated her when she was a little girl because it was the same shape as a scar on her knee. A spread 'M', like a bird flying. Pat had told her it was the Martin trademark. Kes thought it was a kestrel, and Sarah, jealous, had tattooed an M on her knee with a black biro. You could still see it, six years later.

Kes sighed. It was like another life. She stood up and went back inside.

'I hate this. It's like pretending nothing happened. It's stupid. I don't want to do this any more. It's all stupid.' She glared at her mother.

'I agree,' said Kate. 'I give up.' She put down the plate she was holding so hard that it cracked.

The noise was followed by a shocked silence. Mai glared at Kes, started to speak, then suddenly Charlie burst out crying. Big tough Charlie. Charlie who had broken his leg coming off a horse and never even snivelled. He just looked at Finn and started bawling.

Finn put his arms around his father, his eyes filled with tears and his throat closed up. He remembered Kes' insubstantial hand slipping through his, then the force of his grip on her wrist and the unreal flight to the bunker.

Kes heard the explosion over and over again.

She looked up. Her mother was still holding half a broken plate in her hand. Kes rushed around the table and flung her arms around her. 'I'm sorry. I'm sorry. I didn't mean you were stupid. I'm sorry, Mum. I know you were trying to make things good for us. I didn't mean you.'

Her mother stroked her hair. 'Sshh, Kes. It's OK. I never thought you did, my darling Kes. Not for a moment. We are crazy though. It was a dumb idea of mine. No one feels like eating …'

'I do,' said Jack.

'… and we're trying to pretend to have a normal Christmas.'

'So do I,' said Jon.

'Good! Stuff yourselves then!' shouted Sarah. 'Go ahead, the pair of you. Pigs! I'm going to find Angie. No one's thinking about her, are they?' she flung out the door.

Kes started after Sarah but Kate held her. 'She needs some space. Leave her.'

'Good idea,' said Jack quietly.

Charlie's crying had shaken them, broken something loose in everyone.

Sarah found Angie, Emma and the cats hiding in their old cubby under the house and cajoled Angie back inside.

Kate retrieved the Christmas biscuits and mince tarts from the top of the cupboard, but when she lifted down the box, the bottom collapsed and they all fell out. They were sodden too.

It was hopeless. 'We should send out for pizzas,' said Charlie sniffing.

'None of this matters. Nothing,' said Mai firmly. 'The only thing that matters is that there are ten of us here together, safe and unharmed.'

'Right. Mai's totally right!' said Kate. 'Who gives a stuff if the dinner's spoilt. There'll be another Christmas next year.'

We're all safe and we're crying over ridiculous things, thought Kes. Puddings and trucks and burnt jeans. She heaved a sigh. It was like a big spring unwinding in her chest.

'Really, when it's all boiled down,' Pat echoed Mai, 'we're all so damned lucky to be alive and have two houses still standing as a bonus, that the rest is completely unimportant.'

'I declare Christmas dinner finished,' said Mai, piling the untouched plates in front of the twins. 'Here. Go for it.'

The dogs ate the turkey. Emma ate the remnants of the Christmas cake, pudding, biscuits and mince tarts. 'I wanted that pudding, too,' said Jack, with regret.

The verandas were cooler than the stifling house, but the devastation that began beyond them was appalling. Kes tried to avoid looking at the hills, but the smoke spiralling up from the smouldering trees drew her eyes. A tree on the ridge crashed, bursting into flames. Behind her, her mother swore.

Eventually everyone, even the twins, who had eaten an enormous amount, drifted outside.

Charlie and Pat sat on the steps planning tomorrow. They had to get out into the ranges and see if any cattle had survived. Pat was cleaning his rifle. Kes felt sick watching him.

'OK,' said Mai. 'We need to decide a few things. Make some hard choices. It involves all of us, so think about it carefully.'

Kes and Finn's eyes flew to each other. They're going to tell us we have to leave; they both instantly guessed it. Kes saw Finn's face lose colour.

'We've got to talk about what happens next,' said Kate. 'To state the obvious, we're broke. We have a large debt with the bank still to pay off from the drought loan. We'll get some insurance on the farm and maybe some extra government assistance as fire relief, but we'll still be broke at the end of it.'

'What's going to happen to us?' asked Kes. 'What can we do?'

'Find me a river,' said Pat. 'A beautiful flowing river that runs right through the middle of the place. That would be liquid gold right now.'

'And no one's leaving school.' Kate's eyes flashed in that peculiar way when she'd stand no argument, it meant stand clear or be dropped on from a great height. 'So stop thinking about it, you two. I don't want to hear another word about it. What we think we'll do in the short term is this — that is, if you kids agree, because you're our major concern. Yesterday, down in Federation, Mai and I were talking to Eva Grant, the woman who runs the employment agency in

Traralgon. She asked us if we'd need jobs to carry us over for a while — which we certainly will, to have any chance of hanging on here. She has an accountancy job on her books I could have, and work in a nursery that Mai could do with her eyes shut.'

'The trouble is,' said Mai, 'they're both full-time. Pat and Charlie have a huge task cleaning up here and rebuilding fences and shedding. They'll be gone out the back of the range from dawn to dark. Do you think you two, Kes and Finn, with help from Sarah and Angie, could look after the twins over the school holidays while we're at work? If we take the jobs. It'll mean at least eight weeks of two full-time salaries and I don't think we can get by without it.'

'What do you think? All of you?' Mai searched their faces.

'That's what happens now, anyway,' said Jack. 'Everyone who's older than us bosses us round.'

'Yeah. It'll be no different,' agreed Jon.

'Pet lambs!' said Sarah.

'You're the worst, Snake-Eyes,' said Jon.

'But this time you'll have to agree to it and that's not a good way to start,' said Kate. 'It won't work unless you two youngest ones do as Kes and Finn ask. You as well, Sarah and Angie. Kes and Finn will be responsible for all of you during the day.'

'Can we still ride our bikes?' asked Jack.

'Of course. If you don't do stupid things like you did this morning.'

'OK then. But they can't boss us on the weekends or after you get home.'

Kate said, 'I imagine they'll be very glad of the break from "bossing" you. Your father and Charlie will still be here, only they'll be out on the fences most of the time.'

The adults looked at Kes and Finn, waiting for their reply. They looked at each other.

'Of course,' said Finn, speaking for both of them. 'Anything. Anything we can. Anything's better than moving.'

'We're not doing that unless we absolutely have to,' said Kate quickly.

'I won't.' Sarah stood up, defiant. 'I'm telling you now. I don't care what the rest of you do. I'm not leaving. I won't go.'

'It'll be OK. We'll do some good stuff, make some things and go swimming. The water can't have burnt,' Finn said, nodding his head.

Chapter 11

B Y SOME MIRACULOUS turn of wind, the inside curve
of the hill backing the waterhole had escaped the
fire. It was an oasis for the six of them in a charred
desert of destruction and death, deeply blanketed in
grey ash, blurred like an old photograph. By the water,
there was suddenly colour and movement. You could
kid yourself that things were almost normal, if you
didn't let your eyes wander away to the hills.

Kes' eyes always sought the comfort of the water
as they approached. Even at the height of the drought
the waterhole had not run dry — yet. It was tiny now,
compared to the tranquil, meandering stretch of water
it became after the winter rains. Still evaporating and
shrinking, it had become so small Kes could cross it in
a dozen strokes. Most of the time she just floated in it,
thinking.

The billabong was a haven for the wildlife that
had survived. The nesting pair of peregrine falcons had
escaped when the fire ripped across the cliffs of their
ravine, but Kes had not seen the chick, almost fledged
before the fire. She feared it had died.

Each evening hundreds of birds descended on the remaining trees. The white cockies roosted in the flying-fox tree at night. When they arrived in the evening, the tree suddenly blossomed with a thousand screeching white flowers. Every morning as the kids drove up they took off in protesting clouds. Kes worried about where they spent the day and what would happen when their water dried up. She tried to laugh at herself: would she ever get her sense of proportion back?

'The bloody things have wings, Kes,' Finn replied when she told him. 'The rest of their world is still out there unburnt; the birds are far better off than we are, for Christ's sake.'

Tracks of rabbits, foxes, wombats, goannas and emus were clear each morning in the sand. They were all drinking at the waterhole at night, but only the roos hung around the perimeter during the day when everyone was there.

Finn said it was like the Garden of Eden, where all creatures were supposed to have co-existed. Sarah said his mind was wandering.

'Can't you see that this fox ... Finn, look here ... has caught that rabbit there. It's obvious.'

Finn couldn't see anything except scrabbled sand. Sometimes he wondered if Sarah made the whole lot up.

Before the fire, Kes had found a smooth, hand-sized stone in a hollow on the face of the rock wall behind the pool. She believed that the depression in the rock had been a seed grinding site. She loved the stone — it made her think about the unknown ancestors who could have been her people. She liked to sit in the hollow holding it, and dreaming that they might have lived here. Perhaps Rose was wrong and her father was not a Murri, but had come from the Kurnai people, who were the traditional owners of this land.

Kes thought a lot about her father and the Kurnai here. She believed the pool had once been a special place for them and it calmed her down when she worried about what would happen to the families in the wake of the fire.

For long periods of time, she'd sit near the grinding hollow like a hunched bird, staring at the deep water below her, watching the slow progress of a floating leaf or the tiny water-skimmers that skittered across the surface. She could lose herself in that clear brown water, until her mind, wheeling furiously from one thing to another, slowed down and the tension dropped out of her shoulders. Sometimes she could soar above the water like a kestrel, looking down on the pool from above, but that never lasted long, there was always someone to break into her reflection.

Now, floating on the still water, lying on her back on the old air mattress, her hair spreading out like a black halo around her head, she watched the sky warily for smoke, as if she always needed to be prepared for any new disaster. It was ridiculous. They had a 15-

kilometre-wide firebreak all around them, but yesterday she'd seen a cloud low on the horizon that reminded her of smoke, and she'd panicked.

Kes watched the gang-gang cockatoos chewing the blossoms in the trees above her head grow restless, their mechanical mutterings becoming agitated shrieks. The whole flock suddenly lifted out of the tree in a flurry of grey and red, then sped shrieking down the lagoon. Kes squinted up into the sky. A small black dot was hurtling down out of the sun; one of the falcons from the gorge.

Kes saw its claws spread, then, with enough force to break the neck of its prey, knock a bird out of the flock. The two tumbled downwards over her head, until the falcon almost casually scooped up the limp bird from its free-fall and curved away back to the cliffs.

A handful of soft feathers drifted down, settling on the water around her. The grey down was tipped with rose and one of them was stained with blood.

'Did you see that?' Kes called to Finn.

'Yes. Just as it hit. I've never seen that before!'

'They've been timed at 135 ks.'

'You're kidding!'

'No. Some people think they dive even faster,' said Kes, rolling off the air mattress and sinking.

She swam along the clear sandy bottom, watching small water creatures rushing for shelter, as if she truly were the kestrel and they the fleeing cockatoos.

She plucked up a burrowing yabby, amused by its wildly kicking legs.

Was that the way it had been with her father? A small child playing alone by a billabong? Had the troopers come down — one, two, three? Had he been lifted frantic, his two-year-old legs kicking? She flung the creature away from her and came up gasping for air, her heart pounding.

These images racked her brain. She hated it. Increasingly often, waking and sleeping, she couldn't get them out of her mind. It was either the fire, the great wall of flame pushing her down the hill, or these images of her father stolen from his parents. Lifted. Gone forever. Plucked up and abandoned in a strange place.

Could it have been like that, scooped up and kidnapped while he played with his brolga beside some creek? Or was it cold and official, children taken away by tight-faced nurses in starched uniforms, armed with a book of government regulations?

She got out of the water, tears pouring down her face. She had to stop this. She couldn't start crying every time she thought about her father.

'What's wrong? You OK, Kes?' Finn called.

'Yes. Just got a face full of sand off the bottom.'

Finn looked at her, started to speak, then turned away. Why did she lie like that? Even when they were little and she didn't want to, Kes had always talked to him, told him the truth. She was changing, worse, leaving him behind. He started back towards her, but Kes walked away. He felt defeated before he'd started.

Kes had received a reply from Gill in yesterday's mail. She hadn't shown it to Finn, even though he'd seen it when Mai collected the mail. She hadn't even mentioned it because she couldn't talk to him yet. She felt bad on both counts.

Gill had written:

Dear Kes,

I'm glad you live in this imaginary dream when it comes to Greek mountains. I'm telling you, they start to lose their charm when you've chased the bloody goats up and down them for hours, and when you've carted your tenth bucket of water from the well, <u>a long way</u> down the hill. However, if you want to believe I'm living like a movie star in a 5-star hotel, be my guest.

The best part is Granny. She's unique. She thinks I'm dreadful for wearing 'those men's clothes' (my jeans), cutting my hair 'like the boys', not speaking Greek, 'a proper language' and yesterday! Did I cop it! Just as well I couldn't understand her! I got talking to some kids (boys) who live on the farm uphill from us. We could sort of understand each other — we could only speak about ten words of Greek or

English each — but we managed to talk about soccer and some Greek group that's made the charts. (I think) Granny caught me sitting on the gate talking to them, and she pulled me off (she's a head shorter than me but strong as fencing wire) and she dragged me inside by my hair!! She yelled so loudly, she woke Dad up. He just kept laughing and laughing and wouldn't tell me what she was saying. Said it wasn't proper for me to hear it from a grandmother! She yelled at him, too, for not controlling me, I think.

I love her, she's like a little volcano. She must have felt sorry for abusing me, (I suppose that's what she did) because she made that honey cake you love. It took her hours. She wouldn't let Dad have any at first, she smacked him with a wooden spoon! But he got around her, of course. She's so kind, but so fiery! Glad I wasn't Dad when he was a kid!

And no, you aren't going mad. Yes, I do want to hear it — all of it. You don't bore me and I wish like hell I was there, too. Try not to worry too much about not knowing what you're doing. So easy to say! Especially from my 5-star hotel.

I know it's not the same, but remember the six months our family spent in Melbourne when

I was in Year 7? I went to that Catholic girls school in Heidelberg. Well, I felt divided in two as well, only the split wasn't as bad for me. There were two groups, gangs really, at the school, the Anglos and the Wogs. So where did I fit in? Dad's fully Greek. Mum was half and half Irish and Scottish. Jammed in the middle, is the answer. At lunchtime I used to rush out and smoke with the Anglos behind the chapel, then run over and smoke with the Wogs down by the tennis courts. Talk about dying for a cause! It didn't work, of course. The Wogs distrusted me and the Anglos despised me. It was like wriggling on a cactus, every move spikes you until you're a bloody mess. I did that until Maggie Ferguson came. She was all Scottish and wild as. She didn't care about anything or anyone. Hated the lot, except me. It was all right after she came, but for the first three months it was hideous, especially as a West Heidelberg kid in with all the Eaglemont gels. Never knew where my loyalties lay, so, in a pathetic sort of way, I can understand what you're going through.

If it's any help, I think you're very brave. I think you'll do the right thing, because you'd never do anything to hurt your mum or dad. What does Finn think? You didn't say.

As for not knowing things earlier — I don't know about that, Kes. I wouldn't have wanted to know any earlier that Mum was going to die. Shit stuff. You just don't want to know about it. It's impossibly hard when it's as close as your dad. Guessing his pain is worse than feeling your own, I reckon — at least that's how I felt sometimes with my dad. I knew how much I hurt, but I never knew about Dad.

It must've been horrendous for your dad. He's such a gentle man. Maybe he's been trying to hide it from you because he didn't want you hurt too. You can't blame yourself for not knowing things you weren't told. As for you saying you've been living a lie ... it's like calling yourself a hypocrite and that's just bullshit, and you know it.

Kes, I've got to go. There's only one post a week from our little inlet. I can even see the mail boat coming around the headland. Gotta rush! But I heard something about a big fire in east Victoria. Yes, I know it's a big place. Hope it was a long way away. Probably east of Orbost — or in Queensland. No one would know the difference here if it was in New Zealand!

Love to all of you. Tell Finn to write, or he's dead. Much much love,
Gill

I mean it, you're the bravest person I know. XXX
(OK, one X for Finn, but no more unless he
writes. It's what you do with a pen, Finn.)

Kes couldn't get over Gill. It was less than a year
since her mother had died and yet she was calling Kes
brave. Gill was the most extraordinary person to have
for a friend. Even from Greece, she had helped Kes
make a decision about Rose's search.

Sitting beside the waterhole, she wrote two
letters. One was simple.

Dear Rose,

I've spent a long time thinking about everything
we talked about and I've decided that I want
you to contact my grandparents. I hope this is
the right thing to do, but you seem to think so,
so I'd like you to go ahead.

I'm enclosing two other letters with this one.
One is the authorisation. The second one is a
letter to my grandparents, if you ever find
them. I thought they might like to know
something about us. It might help them decide
if they want to contact us. You can read it if
you want. It was so hard to write! It took me
three days and seven starts. Talk about the
worst school essay you ever have to do! The
essay from hell!

You might've heard on the news that we were badly burnt out on Christmas Day. Happy Christmas, I don't think. We're in a pretty bad way now as far as the farm is concerned. We're all worried sick that we'll have to sell up and leave. Not that we have much left to sell! But I hope it doesn't come to that. (That's an understatement!) Sarah's already threatening to keep coming back here and start living in the bush. The trouble is there's no bush left. Just this waterhole, where we spend all our days and which has escaped the fire. Really, it's the only place I feel sane, the rest is like a nightmare.

Anyhow, sorry, this isn't about the fire. Rose, I can't thank you enough for what you're doing for me — us. I just hope Dad will be as pleased as me if you find his family. I think he will be — and if he is, he'll be _really_ pleased. Dad's got this great laugh, I can hear it. When he gets over the shock of it, that is. I'd never do anything that'd really hurt him. I really love my dad, and my mum too, of course.

I hope you had a great Christmas, better than ours!!

Kes Martin

P.S. I forgot. The phone lines all burnt in the fire and the old mobile doesn't work in the mountains. We're getting a mobile that works up here, but we don't have it yet. Could you write to me instead, care of our PO Box at the top of this?

The other one read:

Dear Grandparents,

This will be as big a shock to you as it will be to me if Rose Bannock succeeds in finding you.

My name is Kes (short for Kestrel) Martin and I'm the oldest daughter of Pat Martin, who we think might be your son taken away and sent to Whitehills Orphanage in Melbourne when he was about two.

The first thing I want you to know is that he is very well, forty years old, and a cattle farmer in the Baw Baw Mountains in Gippsland, Victoria. He's the best father in the world and you'd be very proud of him. He's married to my mum, who is also a fantastic person who everyone loves. She's called Kate and she's an accountant when she's not a farmer and mother etc. There are four kids in our family. I'm the oldest, I'm fourteen and not very unusual, all right at school and a really good swimmer. I'm tallish and roundish, I've got a mop of curly black hair and I look Aboriginal. The next is Sarah, she doesn't look Aboriginal (our mum is white), but she's a fantastic tracker. She

knows every animal, bird and beetle on the whole
farm and she knows exactly where everyone is
at any time and what they've been up to —
which is a bit embarrassing sometimes. Sarah's
twelve and she's very beautiful. I think so,
anyhow. She's a real fire-eater, bossy and very
sure of everything, what she's doing and where
she's going.

The last two are twins, Jack and Jon. They're
nine and they're little devils. You can't tell them
apart (that's if they ever stood still long
enough), they're made out of wire and muscle,
with fins and bike wheels instead of arms and
legs, Dad says. They're always in trouble — like
right now (Jon just pushed Jack out of a tree,
and they fell into the billabong). I'm supposed
to be looking after them, but it's almost
impossible! They can't be looked after and they
never take any notice of anyone, least of all
me!

The other half of our family — sorry this is
a bit complicated — are the Lawsons. My mum,
Kate, was Kate Lawson before she married Dad
(your Pat). Mum's brother is Charlie Lawson,
and our two families own this property jointly.
There are two Lawson kids, Finn, my best friend,
who's fifteen and really cool. He's really smart
at school and he's going to be a vet — maybe,

or a cattle farmer here. If we can keep the farm. He's tall and thin and looks Chinese. Sorry, I forgot. Uncle Charlie is married to my auntie Mai who is Chinese. The other Lawson kid is Angie. She's twelve and Sarah's best friend. She doesn't look Chinese and she's deaf, but she lip-reads everything anyone says, and she's a great kid.

We all go to school in Moe, a town near here, and take up half the school bus. It's sixty-five ks to school, but we love living up on the plateau and wouldn't leave for anything.

The four adults in our family are all at work because we've just been burnt out in a bushfire. Dad and Charlie are repairing fences up in the mountains and Mum and Mai are working in the Latrobe Valley, which they hate.

Our property runs herefords — well, it used to, before the fire. It's been in our family for four generations, since 1887. Our closest town is Federation, but you'd never find it on a map, it only has thirty-five people. We're about forty or fifty ks across the mountains from Walhalla, which was a famous gold mining town once, and is on maps. Unfortunately, we don't have any gold here, we could use some right now because we've had a terrible drought for two years and even the bores are running dry. Not that it matters now because all our stock died in the bushfire. However, we were lucky because we were all safe and the two farmhouses, Lawsons' and ours, are still standing.

I don't know what else to write because I don't know if you'll ever get this. It's a bit hard writing to someone, even your grandparents, if you don't know them, so I'm sorry if it's an odd sort of letter. I hope you're interested in all this stuff about us.

What I'd really love is for you to contact us. I'd really love that, but I don't know what it'd be like for you finding someone after thirty-eight years. I'm a bit scared, well, not scared — it's a bit shocking, isn't it, to think we might have another family we don't know about?

I don't know if you'll approve of this bit, but Dad doesn't know about me trying to find you. I know he wants to find you, but he gets so sad when he talks about you that he almost cries … and then he changes the subject. He's tried to find you before, but he's given up, I think. But I haven't, because I'd really like to know my grandparents.

I really hope you contact us, or if you don't want to, just send a message through Rose Bannock and I promise I won't try again, but your kid Pat is the best person in the world, so

I suppose I'm trying to get you to do it. (I hope that doesn't sound like blackmail.)

I hope you had a very happy Christmas and best wishes for the New Year.

Love from your grand-daughter,
Kes Martin

Kes mailed the letter before she got cold feet.

Chapter 12

THE DROUGHT HELD. It was blazing hot by ten o'clock and the hottest days of summer were yet to come. With the red truck a heap of twisted metal, Kes was allowed to drive the ute. The others were delighted, the ute had springs and you could still walk when you got out at the other end. They spent most of their time at the waterhole, away from the devastation. It suited everyone.

Sarah and Angie spent hours out on the claypan, now as dry as the surrounding land, tracking things in the covering of fine ash. Emma lived her days in Angie's shadow or poked around the edges of the swamp, starting in fright at the wild emus that fled at their approach.

The twins were either in the waterhole or on their bikes; a whole new world had opened to them. The fire had cleared out slopes and valleys previously impass-able; now they could even ride through them. Out of everyone, the fire seemed to have affected them least; they were simply irrepressible, tough and resilient in their bodies and their minds.

Finn spent a lot of time reading or staring into space, worrying. Angie often watched her brother, his arms wrapped around his lanky legs, lost in some daydream. She never knew what to say to him at those times. He always replied that he was all right, just thinking about something he'd read or about some friend. Angie knew he was lying, she could see it in his dark eyes, and it made her feel even more remote from him.

Finn couldn't bring himself to tell anyone about his recurring nightmare, even thinking about it made him sweat. It was the same each time he dreamt it and he seemed to dream it almost every night. He was in a barren red desert where one single flower grew out of the sand, a large yellow daisy without leaves. He was always squatting, his hands around it, protecting the flower from the blazing sun. As long as he could shield it with the shade of his body he'd live, if he let the sun wither the flower, he would die too. Sometimes Angie and Sarah were floating there, their arms around each other, like a painting he'd seen at school, but when he tried to speak to them they'd turn away, smiling, trailing a hand towards him. Sometimes he was screaming at Kes, who looked vacantly at him and drifted backwards, flying faster and faster into the sun.

When he woke he'd spend minutes fighting down the panic and the unreasonable anger that he felt towards the three girls. Once he woke in a drenching sweat and realised he'd wet the bed. One day, when he asked Kes if she had nightmares too, she stared at him absently, like she did in the dream, saying, 'What? Sorry, I wasn't listening.' He was so angry with her, he could've hit her.

'I asked you if you ever have nightmares. Tune in, Kes! I'm talking to you!'

Kes gave him a peculiar look. 'All I ever dream about is "Waltzing Matilda",' and walked off.

He'd tried writing a dozen letters to Gill but they sounded so pathetic, like a whingeing kid, that he'd never posted any of them.

One of the things he resented most was being stuck at home looking after the kids when he wanted to be out with his father and Pat on the fences. He craved the hard physical work to get rid of the feeling that he'd explode if he had to sit around wasting time any longer. The last time he'd tried asking his mother was yesterday, she'd snapped at him saying, 'It's too much for Kes to be responsible for all the younger ones on her own. You agreed when you were asked on Boxing Day, Finn. Kate and I have gone to work on that basis. We're all doing things we'd rather not,' she added, a bit more kindly. 'All you kids included. It's hard for the four younger ones to begin to comprehend what might be ahead of them — us.' Finn stopped breathing. 'The most valuable thing you and Kes can do now is to look after them. Really look after them. They need you, Finn.' She searched his face. 'I know it's hard. Believe me, it's bloody hard for us, too, leaving you each morning.'

But he stared her down when she tried to reason further with him, and walked out, slamming the kitchen door.

Finn avoided Mai for the rest of the evening. He knew he'd agreed, jumped at the chance to do something, anything. He knew he was being unfair to Kes, even knew that now he was sulking, but it didn't alter his bottled-up anger. He'd heard Mai and Charlie from his room last night. His father was home late, they usually were, working until well after dark. Charlie's voice was low and angry, Mai would be telling him about their argument.

Then he heard his mother's voice raised, 'For Christ's sake, Charlie! Am I the only rational one left in this house? Angie hardly speaks to anyone and jumps at the slightest sound. She talks more to that bloody emu than she does to me. And she's wetting her bed as well. Sarah's threatening to run away. Kes lives in some dream world. Don't you start on Finn, or I swear I'll move us all into Moe.'

Finn closed his eyes, waiting for the inevitable, but it hadn't come … yet.

'You know it's as hard on them as it is on us. Bite your tongue and be more tolerant. We're the adults.'

Finn looked up. Angie was staring at him. He shut his eyes and put his head back on his knees. He should spend more time with her. His parents were worried about all three girls. He'd get up in a minute and do something with them, get Angie and Sarah to take him out on the swamp. He could pretend to learn some tracks, it was the least he could do. He could feel Angie's eyes boring into the top of his head.

When he shut his eyes, he could see it all as it was before. The ranges covered in tall trees, white trunks peeling bark streamers, the green of the low wattles and callistemon in the scrubby undergrowth with sudden flashes of colour. The silent white faces of the cattle melting into the shadows, the fallen timber, powder-blue new growth on the gums, and the sweet, damp, aromatic carpet of leaves and twigs that crunched underfoot.

His eyes opened against his will. Now all you could see was grey ash over everything, blackened tree stumps, and where the ash had blown off the face of the hills, every small black rock that stood out in silhouette.

Angie was still looking at him with a worried frown.

That morning Angie found the kestrel she'd carved for Kes, lost on the day of the fire. It was embedded in dried mud in the house yard.

'I'll carve you another one, Kes. The wing's broken.'

'No!' Kes said closing her hand over it quickly. 'I want this one. I don't want another. I don't care if it's broken, I like it better.' She turned it over. The backs of the wings were pitted with burn marks, a leg and the tip of one wing was missing. She hung it around her neck. 'There! My luck's back. It was horrible losing it. I don't want another one, this one's — I don't know — it's more real because it's marked by the fire. It's been through the fire and survived, like all of us. There's an Aboriginal creation story about one of the birds rising out of the fire and always carrying the scars of it on its back. It reminds me of that.'

Kes didn't have energy for very much. Behind the waterhole she poked around on the ridges and in the gullies, where she could also think undisturbed, searching around in the rocks, hoping to find other signs of Aboriginal occupation.

That afternoon, on a ridge high above the waterhole, she found a great boulder that had been shattered into hundreds of pieces by the fire. It had a wide vein of quartz running through it, and in the crushed quartz, she found tiny seams of gold.

The twins went mad. Gold fever struck them down instantly and with a lethal dose. While the others were excited and had wild dreams about falling over a footy-sized nugget, the twins were convinced that every rock held a fabulous fortune waiting to be uncovered by them alone.

Angie and Sarah prospected up and down the rock outcrop, finding more snakes and lizards than gold. The twins had a more basic approach. They rode home and brought back a sledgehammer and a masonry hammer from the shed and for the rest of the day, and for many days after, they smashed every rock which they thought looked hopeful.

Kes and Finn soon tired of mining. They wanted the reward without the hard work. Angie and Sarah preferred tracking to breaking rocks, and moved off back to the claypan after the first few enthusiastic days, but the twins didn't give up.

Their property was close to the old Jordan Goldfield of Gippsland where millions of dollars worth of gold had been taken from the Thompson River system and its tributary streams.

'If they could, we can find gold here, too,' the twins insisted every day.

One day they did. Like Kes, they found a split boulder, and cracking it up further, found traces of gold in the quartz seams.

It was as though they were instant millionaires. They speculated about how much the specks were worth, at least a thousand dollars — after all, it was gold — absolutely refusing to believe Pat when he guessed it was worth a dollar or two at the most.

Finding the specks increased their determination to make their fortune. They started to work smarter, only pounding the rocks where a quartz seam showed on the surface.

They read about how to find gold, how to crush rock, about the gold rush in Walhalla, about which rocks bore gold and which didn't. They became quite proficient at telling types of rock and which was potentially gold bearing.

They learnt how to pan for gold and got into strife for sneaking baking dishes from the kitchen for washing pans. They tried to get Finn to build them a puddling machine to grind rocks, driven by old Fred. Finn had buried himself in a new book and said he wouldn't until they found gold properly, then he'd think about it. If he was honest with himself, he didn't have the energy to even consider it.

Jack read about a prospector at Walhalla who, in 1862, had found nuggets lying on the ground. They worked out that their property was on the western edge of the Walhalla geosyncline; the rich gold bearing strip running north from Walhalla through the ranges to Jamieson. Then Jon read in the same book that the mother lode of the alluvial gold in the Jordan River had never been found, even after all those years of prospecting. That was the final straw. The Jordan was not far from their property as the crow flies. The twins became full-time, dawn-to-dark prospectors.

Kes was amazed at their persistence. Every day she loaded up the back of the ute with towels, hats, lunches, books, Angie and Emma, Sarah and her plastering equipment, for taking castings of animal tracks, goggles and snorkels for herself and Finn, the twins with their bikes and prospecting gear, backpacks, spades, hammers and all their other bits and pieces.

Every morning the others listened to descriptions of the nuggets that the twins would definitely find today. Kes and Finn rode in the cabin, feeling like the parents of a totally weird bunch of kids.

The twins roamed up and across the ranges. They couldn't get lost, they knew every inch of the property and most of their neighbours' land as well. They came back to be fed at lunchtime, then disappeared again until five, when Kes and Finn had to get home and start preparing the evening meals.

Each night the twins rode home exhausted, ate and dropped into bed. The next day, when the sun came up, they were awake. Kes could hear them from her room planning the day's prospecting. As soon as they reached the waterhole, they were off and at it again. She waited for the enthusiasm to wear off but it never did. Every five or six days, they'd find a speck of gold in something and this would spur them on.

One night, Kate spoke to them at dinner when they were dropping asleep in their food, 'You're not trying to save the property single-handed, are you?'

'No, Mum.'

'You are doing this just for fun, aren't you?'

'No!' said Jack, indignant. 'We're going to find a heap of gold.'

'So we can get more cattle and pay off the bank,' said Jon.

Kate sighed. 'Yes, that's what I mean. Just do it for fun, OK? Don't worry about the cattle.'

'It's not fun. We're prospecting.'

'And we're going to find a heap of gold.'

'Did you know that in the gold rush in Jericho, down on the B.B. Creek where it joined the Jordan, this old bloke Grogan found four nuggets on his claim that were over thirty ounces each? The biggest was eighty-two ounces,' said Jack. 'Gold's worth $350 an ounce, that's $28,700 now, just for the big one!'

'And down on the Jericho someone found one that weighed 117 ounces.'

'Why did they call it B.B. Creek?' asked Pat.

The twins rolled around laughing. Jack said, 'The book says that the miners were so tattered and torn that their bare bollocks showed out of their trousers.'

'What's a bollock, Dad?' asked Jon.

Kate looked at Kes and shook her head. It was useless. They had gold fever as badly as any of the original miners; Kes had already told her that. It would wear off.

There were steps on the veranda, then Finn's exasperated voice. 'Go on, Mum. You did it, you own up to it. Tell them. Go inside.'

Then Charlie's big laugh. 'You're in trouble, Mai.'

Finn led Mai into the Martins' dining room, holding her wrist as if she was naughty child. Mai looked as if she'd been caught stealing.

'Go on, Mum, tell them what you just did.'

'Don't be silly, Finn, you're making a mountain out of a molehill.' Mai shook herself free.

'What've you done, Mai?' Pat gave her his chair. 'Sit here and confess.'

'I've just had a phone call from Stella Conway, Brian's mother,' Mai said. 'Brian's father has gone into hospital suddenly. He's had a major heart attack and Stella is frantic.'

Kes groaned, 'You didn't, did you?'

Finn nodded, 'She did.'

Mai glared at them both. 'Brian has been talking constantly about you kids since he went home — heaven knows why, with that attitude. His mother said he had a wonderful weekend, the time he stayed here.'

'Lying little hound,' Sarah snapped.

'Stella has asked if Brian could stay just for a few days. He's very anxious about his father and Stella feels that if he could get away from home for a short while, he might be able to distract himself.'

'Distract us, you mean,' said Finn. 'Me particularly. I get him in my room.'

'How long's a short while?' Sarah asked.

'Four days.'

'Sounds like an eternity to me.'

'Did she know we'd been burnt out?' Pat asked.

'No, she was really shocked.'

'But she still asked if Brian could come?' Kate said.

Mai nodded.

'What a peculiar woman,' Kate added.

'So you agreed?' Kes shook her head at her aunt. 'Mai, you're so hopeless. I hope no one ever asks you for Charlie, you'd hand him straight over.'

'Don't be ridiculous, Kes. I'm not foolish. I think the boy has a genuine need. I don't think things are happy for him at home. I don't think his parents get on that well together. Even though it wasn't easy for him here last time, Stella assures me he's asking to come back. He's very positive about it!'

'I can't stand that snobby kid,' said Jon. 'He's a big wanker.' Kate frowned at him. 'He said our bikes were crap, Mum!'

'I'd have thought he'd need to be with his mother,' Pat said.

Mai glanced up, 'Do you think I've done the wrong thing? Stella was crying on the phone, so upset, so worried about both of them, it was hard to say no.'

'Carry that new mobile with you, Charlie, or God only knows what you'll be sold if the salesman cries,' Pat said. 'But I don't know, Mai, he seemed pretty unhappy last time he was here. Are you sure he wants to come?'

'Doesn't he have other family?' Charlie asked. 'We hardly know the kid.'

'Dad! I know him!' Angie shouted at her father.

Kes sighed. 'He was fine. We were the ones who were unhappy. Bloody hell! We'll have the little toad for weeks, I know it in my bones.'

'A few days …'

'Shut up, Kes!' Angie's face lit up with anger. 'You don't know anything. So just shut up about him! He's my friend and I like him. I like him a lot. He's really good to me in hospital; he invents these crazy games to play and he reads to me. Every night. The nurses used to let him come and talk to me when all the little kids were asleep and my ears were hurting. You don't know anything about him, you just like to criti-cise and make judgements and you know nothing! Nothing! You never listen to the things I say about him. None of you do. It's just a game to you — what smart comments can you think up about Brian that'll make you sound clever.'

'It's OK, Angie…' Kes started.

'It's not OK. You're all horrible to him. You're being smart-arses. You think it's funny. You've got no idea what he thinks because you never tried to find out. It's not funny. It was his dad that used to come and visit him. His mother only came once last time we were in, only once in the whole thirteen days. His father might die and you're just thinking about yourselves.'

'Sorry, Ang.'

'I think he should stay as long as he wants. I'll look after him. I think you're all selfish and disgustingly self-centred. Anyhow, Mum's picking him up from the train after work tomorrow, so shut up all of you, or suffer.'

'I will,' said Kes, under her breath.

Chapter 13

THE NEXT MORNING the twins loaded their miners' gear onto the back of the ute. Today they planned to prospect the ridge and ravines directly west of the waterhole. Sarah and Angie were coming with them for the morning. They wanted to see what creatures had survived the fire in the gullies behind the lagoon.

It was new territory for all of them. The gorge they were heading for had been an overgrown fern gully before the fire, with sides too steep to allow easy access, even for the cattle. The beasts avoided it and it became an impassable jungle of fallen wood and deep, wet vegetation. The kids knew it was there but could never penetrate the mish-mash of fallen wood that hid the valley floor, or the dense vines and ferns that formed an impenetrable canopy over it. But the vegetation had dried out in the two years of drought, and the fire, ravaging the cliffs and gully floor, razed all of the ferns, the lower scrub and most of the fallen ground cover. The twins said it now looked possible to walk through the gutted ravine along the gully floor — still difficult with burnt-out and fallen tree trunks, but passable.

The twins and Sarah and Angie topped the ridge above the valley mid-morning. The girls sat on the edge looking down into the ravine; the twins surveying the rock walls for likely gold seams.

'I reckon I can see a vein of quartz coming down the side of the big crack, near that big orange patch of rock,' said Jon, showing off in front of Sarah. 'What do you think, Jack? Good place to start?'

Jack nodded, searching for footholds down the cliff face. Against the blackened trunk of an ancient fallen giant, he found a rough sort of rock cascade, used as an animal track and firm enough to scramble down. He slid down the rocks, calling out to the girls, 'Follow us and you'll be all right.'

Sarah and Angie smiled at each other. Sarah shook her head, 'I was petrified ... you too?'

'Keep us in sight,' ordered Jon.

'Oh yeah, sure,' said Sarah, 'otherwise it's dead certain we'll get lost. You can only see the houses, the swamp and the waterhole from here. And your great clumping feet are making tracks like dinosaurs.'

'OOooohh! Great Snake-Eyes speaks.'

The girls scrambled down the valley wall after the twins. The floor of the gully was deeper than it appeared from the ridge and twisted and turned along its length like an old river bed, although there was no sign now of water. It was filled with soft grey ash that puffed up at every step, covering them in a grey film. Emma scratched around under every log that had survived, finding insects and the occasional green shoot.

'Life's tough, eh?' said Angie. 'Survive the fire and get eaten by an emu.'

The twins disappeared around a bend, still chattering about gold seams. The girls dawdled behind looking for signs of life.

'There's not much here. A few birds. Some lizards. Lots of them actually, I think they like it here after the fire. But that's all.'

'Oh look, Sarah, isn't that sad?' The stiff body of a wombat lay on its back near a hole in the bank.

'Didn't make it home in time. Or maybe it was smoked out of its burrow.'

'Poor thing.' Sarah shuddered. That's what would've happened to Kes and Kate and Finn if they hadn't got to the bunker in time. She looked away quickly — she couldn't afford to let thoughts like that creep into her mind. They took over too fast.

'Look, here's another. Or is it a koala? Too burnt to tell. This is horrible, Sarah.'

'Yeah. I wish we hadn't come this way.'

They walked up the gully quickly, away from the dead creatures. Clouds of ash rose around them, settling in their hair and on their clothes.

'You look ancient, Sarah. You've got grey hair.'

'You look like a ghost. You're grey, top to bottom.'

'It must've been lovely before the fire though. It's chock-full of burnt tree-fern trunks.'

'At least these huge old gums will grow again. I don't know about these ferns though. Do they recover from fire? How long does it take before wombats and emus can come back to live in a place this burnt?'

'I suppose when it gets rain and the grass grows. There are a couple of orchids over here, but nothing else will grow in this without water. It's like the moon it's so dead.'

Angie sat on a rock and looked up at Sarah, pain on her face. 'It's like my dream,' she whispered. 'I dream it all the time. The whole world's been burnt, there's a grey smoking valley, like this one, and it's blazing hot. We're all walking somewhere in this dead place and you keep saying, "We have to go back, we've lost the twins." I always say, "No, we can't, they're not really lost." But they never come when you call and when we find them they're dead because I wouldn't go back. It's horrible. I can't get it out of my head.'

'Angie! It's OK. It's only a dream.' Sarah sat on the boulder beside her. 'It's not real, Ang. You'd always go back for them, you know that.'

'But what if I was too scared? If a fire was coming, I'd be too scared.'

Sarah didn't know what to say, except, 'You're the bravest of us all, Ang. You'd always do something brave if you needed to. I'm more of a big-mouth, but you're the bravest one. Think of all those horrible operations and all that time in hospital on your own.'

'Do you have bad dreams?'

'I can't remember my dreams. I just know they're awful. Do you think we'll ever stop having night-mares?'

'I don't know. We'll be OK, won't we, Sarah?'

Down the gully, the boys were chipping rocks.

'I hope so. We have to be.'

Angie looked around for Emma, who had disappeared. 'The boys never give up, do they? They'll probably find something one day — they deserve to. Where did Emma go this time? I was just looking at her and she vanished again. She was on that rock face between those two huge boulders.'

'Call her, Angie.'

'Emma. Emma. Emma! Where are you, bird brain? Emma. Emma!'

'There she is!' said Sarah. 'She just appeared out of that wall of rock again. That's funny, I was looking straight at that rock and she appeared out of it like magic. What is it? There must be a crack in the rock we can't see from here.'

The girls jumped over the fallen tree trunks to the rockface.

The far side of the ravine was a solid rock wall except for a wide split, which rose up two metres above their heads. A recess in the rockface camouflaged the crack until you were in front of it. Sarah dragged Angie up the last ledge as Emma scurried past them inside the opening again, pecking at pale insects in the half light.

'Angie! Look in here! Look at this! It's deep in there. Come out here, Emma, you'll get lost!'

'What!! What's in there? This is unreal! Is it a cave? Do you think it is, or just a fault in the rock? It looks pretty dark and deep from out here.'

'I'll call the twins.' Sarah bellowed down the gully, 'Jon! Jack! Come quick! Quick. Run! We've found a cave, we think.' She stuck her head inside again, squinting in the half darkness.

'Come on, hurry up. It's huge!' Angie yelled.

The twins raced back up the creek bed. 'Did you find gold? Have you found gold?' they shouted, leaping over the fallen trees and scrambling up onto the ridge.

'No, it's a cave! It's fantastic! Look in here!'

Jack stuck his head in. 'Geez! It's enormous! A real one!' he said in awe. 'It echoes.'

'Give us a look. Shove over, Jack. Cool! How did you find it? Can we go in?'

'Yeah! At least, I suppose so,' said Angie. 'We'd better be careful though. We don't know what's in there. I mean, the roof might cave in on us.'

'There could be holes in the floor, too,' said Jon with authority, opening his pack and pulling out a torch. 'We always carry a torch.'

For once no one laughed at their complete miners' prospecting kit. Jon stuck his head inside and shone the torch around. 'The roof's solid rock. So's the floor. This is wicked!'

The four of them squeezed through the entrance

crack cautiously. Inside, it was cool and dry. A large cavern twisted away deep into the hill. Their voices echoed off the walls.

'Fantastic!' said Angie. 'This is the best thing ever.'

'Awesome!' shouted Jon, the word bouncing back around their heads. 'Awesome, awesome, awesome.'

'It's ancient. I bet no one's ever been in here before. We've found something no one's ever seen before. It's like finding a new land,' said Sarah.

The walls of the cave were smooth and clean. 'No worries about the roof,' said Jack, flashing his torch over it. 'It's solid. This is so cool! I can't believe we've found a cave!'

'It's smooth, like it's carved out by water. Kes'll tell us how. She knows about rocks.'

They took a few steps deeper into the cave. Only a few metres away from the door, the soft light was already fading away to almost nothing. About ten steps from the entrance, where the weak light gave out completely and they needed the torch to penetrate the darkness, the cavern narrowed into a tunnel.

'If you're going to keep the torch, Jon, stay close to me,' Angie said. 'I'll need it to see your faces or I won't understand a word.'

For some reason, Emma was frightened by the cave, and refused to follow them beyond the mouth. She seemed to be scared of its dark recesses and wouldn't venture further, even with Angie.

The air chilled at the entrance to the tunnel, and the sounds from outside faded under a cold blanket of silence. They walked cautiously along the passage, feeling the walls, Jon leading them with his torch.

The air smelled old, as if nothing had breathed it for a thousand years. Their feet sounded unnaturally loud in the narrow passage, and they could hear each other breathing, faster than normal. Those were the only sounds; even the twins were silent.

About thirty metres from the cave mouth, the tunnel branched into a 'Y'. Two passages, slightly narrower than the one where they stood, ran into blackness to the right and left. Jon shone the torch down the right-hand one.

Where the torchlight gave out, they could see it curving away, a twisting rocky tube. There was just enough room for the four of them to stand, hunched over, in the fork.

'Should we go on?' asked Angie, her eyes showing white and large in the torchlight.

'We can't stop now,' said Jon, starting along the left branch.

Sarah grabbed his shirt as he took off. 'Stop, Jon! You idiot. You can't go charging off like that. You can get lost if you want, but I'll keep the torch thanks.'

'Keep up then. You sound like Kes. Come on.'

The left tunnel narrowed and the roof lowered to brush the tops of their heads. As they tentatively walked along, it narrowed again to single file width for another twenty metres.

'This is really spooky,' said Jack. 'Do you reckon there's anything in here?'

'Give us your torch,' said Sarah, and flashed it around the floor; it was smooth but dusty. In parts water had run through, leaving a smear of cracked clay. 'I don't think so, no sign of any tracks. Anyway it'll only be a wombat.'

'How can you tell, Snake-Eyes? You wouldn't know — it's all solid rock. Anyway, I don't want a wombat charging us. They've got bloody big claws.'

'Don't worry about it, Jack,' said Sarah, more confidently than she felt. 'And don't ask questions if you don't like my answers.'

It *was* spooky, walking along single file, deep inside the hill. Sarah felt very closed in, particularly if she thought of the tonnes of rock above them. She felt for Angie behind her and took her hand. Angie squeezed it, she always knew what she was thinking. Of all of us in here, Ang is the one with the most guts, Sarah thought. The rest of us act as if we're not scared, but if the worst happened, it'd be her who'd get us out. The thought of being lost in the cave suddenly sent a wave of pure terror through Sarah. She stopped abruptly, gasping for breath. Her hands broke out in a sweat and her heart thumped as if someone was jumping on her chest. She clung onto Angie's arm.

'Stop for a minute, please Jon,' said Angie calmly.

'What's the matter?'

'Give me your torch for a minute. I just trod on Sarah. She's lost her shoe.' She squatted down, peering at Sarah's face in the half light of the torch. 'Are you OK?'

'Sorry,' Sarah whispered, gasping, 'I just got into a panic all of a sudden. I was all right, then I thought about the rock above us. It only lasted for a second. I'm OK now.'

'We're only going on for another few minutes,' said Angie to the twins, 'then we'll go back and get the others. All right?'

'No way ...' Jon started to complain.

Angie shone the torch on him. 'Yes! Bird brain. Only one more bend then we're going back. Anyhow, I can hardly see anyone's face with this little torch. I'm finding it really hard even to talk to Sarah.'

Almost immediately the passage widened into a little bubble, then burst out suddenly into a large cavern.

'Geez! Look at that!'

'Don't yell like that, Jack. You scared the hell out of me,' said Sarah, her heart pounding again.

Jon grabbed the torch and flashed it around. It was bigger than the first cave. The walls curved up to a domed roof six metres above their heads. High on one wall a row of huge holes hung above a metre-wide rocky ledge, like round windows on a stone balcony. They couldn't see where they went; the space behind them gave out into blackness.

'Unbelievable!' said Angie. 'They look as if someone's carved them out!'

Jon swung his torch around slowly. 'What's that?' he said suddenly.

'Jon, for Christ sake! Stop scaring me.'

'Oooo, scaring Snake-Eyes!' he said, holding the torch under his chin and making ghost noises.

'Stupid and not funny,' Angie said sharply. 'You've more than worn out that dumb joke. Here, do something useful, give me back your torch. I can't see what anyone's saying.'

'Ang, shine it down there,' said Jack.

The light showed another passage, then another, then a third. One curved away on ground level, one sloped down sharply from the level of the cave floor and the third, with an opening about a metre up the wall, led off into the darkness again.

'We're not going down any of those tunnels,' said Sarah loudly.

'Aaaw, Sarah! Snake-Eyes is scared!'

'Shut up, Jack,' Angie ordered, 'and cut out the Snake-Eyes crap. I'm sick of it. I mean it. I don't care. You can bleat all you want. You're not going. These caves could go on forever. After a few twists and turns and another cavern or two, where are you then, hey?'

'Buried alive,' added Sarah in support, 'and then your torch goes out.'

Jon opened his mouth. 'No!' Sarah shouted at him, 'Listen to Angie, you idiots! We're doing it properly. We're going to get Kes and Finn right now. We've got to get torches and ropes and cord and things to find our way out again — and stuff to make maps as well. This place is a maze. The whole hillside could be a honeycomb. Who knows where these tunnels go? Or what's further in? Turn around, Jon, we're out of here.'

Sarah marched the twins, protesting, back down the tunnels in front of her.

Chapter 14

Finn was up in the flying-fox tree mending the twins' latest doomed attempt at flight. He was planning the letter he'd promised to write to Gill. He missed her more than he'd thought he would. He missed them both, Gill and Kes. Gill'd be able to tell him how to talk to Kes. He could hear her laughing at him, 'You open your mouth, Finn, waggle your tongue and words come out.'

Below him, Kes floated, watching the patterns of the leaves against the sky. She was thinking about what Mai had said to her last night. 'It's not a question of what you half are, it's more the old question of whether a glass is half full or half empty.'

With a confidence that Kes wished she possessed, Mai had added, 'You've always been a half-full not a half-empty type of person.'

Kes had passed it off, laughing, 'That's the twins. They're never more than half full even after a huge meal.'

Mai had looked at her searchingly. 'It's never easy, Kes. It's hard enough just being nearly fifteen and deciding who you are, let alone coming to terms with your culture, and working out where you fit into that as well. It's like a journey that you're on before you know you've started.'

'And you didn't even ask to go in the first place,' Kes had complained.

'Now don't give me that nonsense. It's exciting to sort out where you're going and how you're going to travel. What sort of philosophy you're going to live by. It's a challenge to everyone ... all through their lives actually. It doesn't stop, you know.'

'I don't even know what philosophy means, Mai, let alone where I'm going, and I don't think it's exciting. Mostly it makes me cry.'

'Rubbish. You're much tougher than that, and philosophy is what people think about things; their values, ideas, spirituality, right and wrong, good and bad. Finn's ethics, all those things that make us individuals and different from the mob. You have the added advantage of two cultures, just as I did, as Finn and Angie have; most people in Australia only have a Western Christian cultural heritage. We're the lucky ones.'

'That's the problem,' Kes had answered angrily, 'What culture? I don't know what the hell I am and I don't know the first thing about my culture, except bits I learnt at school and that was as foreign to me as it was to Gill Papadopolous. Those classes were so embarrassing I could have crawled out the window. Everyone kept looking at me, asking questions and deferring to me … as if I knew anything. I knew nothing. Nothing! Dad won't talk about it. He says he doesn't remember, and doesn't know, but that's bullshit. He must remember stuff, and he can't have lived this long without finding out something about his own culture. You just can't just go through life being Aboriginal and keep your eyes that tightly shut.'

Mai looked at her for a long time, opening and closing her mouth, before she finally answered. 'Kes, Pat has made very hard choices in his life. You're old enough to understand that his early life was abysmal, parts of it were very brutal. He had a … a hideous childhood and teenage years, probably right up until the time he met Kate. I know a little of it, only what he's chosen to tell me. Kate knows more, of course, but even she says she doesn't know the full extent of the abuse he suffered as a little child, and then as a teenager, which might've been even worse for a sensitive young person like your dad. He was only a year older than you, Finn's age, when he ran away from Gibson's farm and got that job on the railways.

'He'll tell you what he chooses, but if he doesn't that's his right. His business. He may possibly tell you more as you get older. But he may never.'

'I'm old enough. I can understand what you're saying. I understand how hurt he was as a kid. I can't imagine having to run away and start from scratch supporting myself though — I mean, how'd you eat? Where'd you sleep?'

'He said he stole, begged, slept on the streets and used the Salvos.'

Kes shivered.

Mai smiled at her. 'It's not a matter of being old enough, Kes. None of us think of you as children, you've all been through far too much in the last few weeks. It's a matter of allowing Pat to make the choice of what he wants to tell you and respecting the reasoning, or just the plain pain, that drives that decision. Your father suffered as a teenager from the very worst of Australian redneck racism. Whether it's right or wrong, he'll never forget what he's trying to protect you from. Not everyone wants to talk about things that are very painful to them … and when they do, they choose their own time.

'I'm telling you things you already know, Kes, but let me remind you of something. You know last year when Gill's mother was killed, you didn't sit by her and badger her to tell you how she felt.'

'No. She felt like shit, that was obvious.'

'What did she want from you?'

'I don't know. Most of the time I felt useless.'

'What I saw you do was to judge when she wanted you and to be with her those times. She probably couldn't even have said if she wanted your conversation or just your body there for comfort. That's what close friends do. You're a close friend to your dad.'

Kes said slowly, 'Yeah, I guess I am. I still think of myself as his kid. He's my dad, I'm his kid.'

'The best thing that can ever happen to parents is that their kids grow up to be their friends. Which doesn't mean that you won't cop it if you burn your jeans again like you did on Boxing Day.'

Kes nodded. 'God, that was a horrible day, wasn't it? Everyone wandering around like lost souls.' Her eyes suddenly filled with tears. 'That's what it would've been like for Dad, wouldn't it? I get sick thinking about that. I have such horrible nightmares about it. I can't imagine being without all of us. What would I do without Finn? Or any of them, even those bloody twins, who drive me nuts most of the time. It wouldn't just have been where to sleep or what to eat, would it? It would've have been being totally alone with no one to care for, or to care about you.'

'That's why Kate, you four kids, and our extended family are so important to him. We're the most precious things in his life. Pat and Kate are quite extraordinary people to draw out of the lucky dip of parents. Two people from widely different backgrounds and circumstances who've created a loving partnership for themselves and a great family for you kids.'

Kes's air mattress bumped gently into a sunken tree, breaking her train of thought. She watched a flock of white cockatoos fly into the tree above her, turning this conversation over and over in her mind, wondering if optimism was enough to work it all out.

Outside the cave, the world suddenly turned hot and blinding-bright. Sounds and colour returned to the world.

'It's like coming out from the underworld,' said Sarah. 'Like that Egyptian myth of the sun god. What was his name? Ra? He lived underground at night and brought the sun out in the morning.'

'Yeah, right, Sa-Ra. Ra, Ra, Ra, for you, too,' said Jack. 'Come on, Jon, let's go. She'll reckon she can make the sun rise next.'

The four scrambled across the black tree trunks on the valley floor and climbed back up the gorge wall. They ran the kilometre back to the waterhole and crashed down the bank in an avalanche of ash and tumbling rocks.

'What's the matter?' Kes sat up quickly and fell off her air mattress. 'What's happened?'

Finn swung down out of the tree, 'For Christ's sake, what's wrong?'

For a second no one could speak, then they all started shouting together.

'We've found a cave!' 'Emma found a cave.' 'We've found passages that go on forever into the hill.' 'It's fantastic, there are tunnels and caves and ...' 'There's a cave, two caves, one's as big as a house, bigger, much bigger and we don't know what's down the passages.' 'You have to come and look. It's amazing.'

'Sarah got scared.' 'It's like nothing else and no one's ever been there. It's awesome.' 'It's really spooky.'

Kes and Finn looked at them in amazement.

'Where?' asked Finn. 'You're crazy. There aren't any caves here. We've never seen anything like that. Are you sure?'

'Of course we're sure,' said Jon. 'We went inside and down a tunnel to a ginormous cave, but then Angie and Sarah made us come out. It's just fantastic, Finn! Kes! You've got to come and look.'

'OK! We're coming! Wait till I get my runners on. I can't believe you! You're not pulling my leg, are you?' Kes asked sharply.

'No, Kes. Honestly, you can be so dumb. It's really huge and it goes on and on, down all these tunnels.'

Kes and Finn threw some clothes on and scrambled up the hill, along the ridge and down into the gully floor.

'Now stop here,' said Sarah. 'Look up there and guess where the cave mouth is.'

'I've no idea,' said Finn.

Angie said, 'That's why we've never found it, it's hidden from down here, but now the fire's cleared the entrance. The gorge was choked with dead wood and fallen trees, full of ferns and undergrowth before. It's up there, behind that edge. Emma found it. She just appeared out of that wall when I called her.'

They led the other two up to the ledge and into

the first cavern. Finn and Kes, dumbfounded, gazed around in astonishment.

Sarah asked, 'What's made it, Kes: is it water? It's so smooth and sculptured, it looks like the stones in the river. Worn smooth.'

'The water's scoured it out. It's taken the insides out of the hill,' Finn said.

Kes agreed, 'Yeah sure, it's water-carved all right. But how? And when? There's no sign of water now. It must've been millenniums ago. It'd take that long to gouge out these walls. It's certainly been part of an ancient river system, but it's been underground by the look of the roof. That's carved out, too, water-worn, just like the cavern.'

'I can't believe this's been here all this time and we've never found it,' said Finn, slowly turning in circles. 'It's like the caves you find on the beach, worn smooth by the sand and waves. What a fantastic find!'

'But wait till you see the tunnels and the other cave,' said Sarah.

Already ahead, Jon called back, 'Come and look here.' He flashed his torch into the tunnel. 'This is unreal down here.'

'Jon! Wait for us!' Kes said sharply.

They felt a bit more confident going down the tunnel a second time. Kes and Finn followed Jon, who guided them with the torch, while the other three walked in the darkness behind feeling their way along the walls.

When they reached the point where the passages branched, Finn gasped. 'There's another one! Where does that go?'

'We told you! There's a whole lot of them,' Jon's voice echoed. 'We haven't been down there yet. They wouldn't let us. Come on. This way.'

He led them along the long winding passage and then stood aside quickly as it broke out into the big cavern.

'Fantastic!' cried Kes.

'It's bloody unbelievable,' said Finn. 'Look! There are more tunnels over there.'

'Sarah said we weren't allowed to go into them until we had proper equipment. She said we'd be lost forever. But she was scared, both of them were.' Jack hoped Kes would let them.

'Can we go now?' asked Jon.

'What down there? With one little torch? Are you mad? No way! No way at all!' said Kes quickly. 'Good on you, Sarah. you're dead right. No one goes anywhere in here without all sorts of safety precautions. Do you all promise me? Very seriously, promise me. Cave systems like this can go for kilometres. People get lost in them, even experienced cavers. We've no idea where any of this goes. Do you all promise?'

'OK, Kes,' said Jon. 'You don't have to go on and on, we get the message.'

'That's why we came back to get you, and to get stuff for exploring,' Jack added.

'Tomorrow. We'll come back with all the gear tomorrow,' Kes said.

'Kes, on the way back, can we go a little way down the other passage, where they branch, just a short way? It's straight back to the entrance, even if the torch gave out we could feel the walls,' said Angie. 'I'm dying to see if it runs out or if it goes somewhere.'

Kes and Finn looked at each other. Kes hesitated, she was desperately curious and trying to weigh up her responsibility against that curiosity.

Finn said, 'OK, if Kes agrees, but only a short way, a very short way, and no side passages or anything. As soon as we come to a branch we're going back.'

They retraced their steps until they met the 'Y' branch in the passage. Kes didn't know if she was scared at the risk they were taking, or so excited that she couldn't breathe properly. They walked along the right-hand tunnel slowly, in single file, again following Jon's light.

'God, I hope this is OK,' said Finn quietly to Kes.

The passage twisted, turned, and seemed to go on forever, running smooth and flat, the walls curving in and out over their heads. The deeper into the hillside they went, the colder it became, until they were shivering in their light T-shirts.

Finn called a halt, 'I think we've gone too far. We need a back-up light. It's too dangerous just having one torch.'

'Just one more bend,' pleaded Jon, 'Please, just one more. I've been watching the walls and they're widening out. One more, then we'll stop.'

Finn flashed his watch on, the soft blue light lighting up his face. 'Two minutes by this watch from now. Not a second more. One more bend, no more, and no arguing.'

As suddenly as before, the passage turned sharply and opened out into a cavern. It was enormous, far bigger than the one they had just come from. A house — two houses — could fit into it. The six of them stood in stunned silence.

'What is it?' whispered Angie, squeezing Finn's arm. 'Give me the torch, Jon, I can't see anyone without it.'

The great roof was festooned with a thousand finger-thin stalactites, hanging down like twisting, icy roots. An upside-down landscape, a hanging forest, through which strange things might wander.

Angie said, 'It's like a thousand hands are grabbing for you.'

'Look! There's stuff painted on the walls!' said Sarah.

Although the roof was extraordinary, it was the walls that created turmoil in Kes. In a continuous band around the oval cave, human handprints leapt to life in the light of the torch.

Angie realised she'd been holding her breath. 'What is it?' she asked again.

'It's the most amazing place I've ever seen,' whispered Kes. 'And we're the first people ever to see it, for hundreds of years, maybe thousands.'

'It's like the Buchan caves,' said Sarah, 'but better, much much better. Look at that thing!'

On the far side of the cave, watching the entrance from which they had just emerged, a thin black figure with a fantastic plumed headdress stared at them from concentric, white-circled eyes. It was painted on the wall over another tunnel.

'It's guarding the entrance,' said Kes. A black passageway curved away into the darkness beyond the reach of the torchlight. She could hardly speak. She felt as if the spirits of a thousand generations of her people were here, almost as if she had found them, or they had found her.

She walked across to the handprints and gently placed her hand over one. It was a perfect fit. She stood there smiling, as if, in the absolute silence of the cave, the walls were talking to her. If she could only understand enough, open some part of her brain that felt shut, she'd hear them, all the old people, the ones who had been here before.

Of course, they weren't the first ones to find this cave. The Kurnai people had lived in these mountains for thousands of years. This must have been a special place for them. Kes could almost feel them standing beside her. It was quiet, like the silence inside a big cathedral, cool like one as well. In the light of the torch the hands danced and flickered across the rock face. This is how things would have looked in the flames of the burning sticks that had given the painters their light.

She looked at the floor. In the centre were the charcoal remains of ancient fires. Kes felt like crying. It was as if she'd come here just too late and missed them. The small campfire remains were such a familiar sight, like the hundreds of fires their own families had sat around out bush when they went camping. It felt as if her family had got up and walked out of the cave without waiting for her.

The others were watching her. She felt Sarah put her arm around her. 'It's wonderful, isn't it?' Sarah whispered, 'and sad. I wish they were still here. I wish they all hadn't gone. I wish we could talk to them.'

Sarah knows; she understands it, thought Kes. I'll talk to her about this tonight, when the kids are in bed. She's always clear and certain about things. Kes hugged her.

Even the twins were quiet. They felt their way over to the far side and peered into the hole guarded by the black figure. Kes was uncertain of what she should do. She felt that they shouldn't be trespassing in this place.

The twins were looking down the entrance that led from the cave. 'It's another passage going on. It slopes down. It's pitch black in there,' said Jon.

'No!' said Finn suddenly. 'We're not going any

further. We're not equipped. We're relying on this one torch and it's starting to look dim. We're going out right now. Brian's coming this evening, too.'

Everyone, except Angie, had completely forgotten him. Kes groaned, 'Great.'

'Shut up, Kes!' Angie flared up. 'Don't you start again.'

'I'll try to behave.'

Angie gave her a dirty look.

'Come on, Jack and Jon, in front of me.' Finn gave Kes a sympathetic look, not missed by Angie. 'Kes, will you go last? Make sure everyone stays in front of you.'

Finn marshalled them up quickly, suddenly anxious, as if they'd been stretching their luck too far. They filed back silently into the passage leading out to the cave mouth.

Kes turned and looked back at the thin figure on the far side of the cave with its bright white eyes and wild plumes. It was staring at her as she turned away. Was it the all-powerful Bunjil spirit she'd learned about? Was that the west wind he'd captured blowing around his head?

She felt his eyes boring holes in her back. She'd remember that stare as long as she lived.

On the way home, they decided to keep the cave a secret from their parents, and also from Brian.

Kes and Finn were torn up about it. They all knew their parents would be worried sick about them exploring the cave system on their own. In fact, the older two were certain that they'd be banned from ever going into it again on their own, their parents would have to be with them. And that meant only on weekends, and even then it'd happen only if their parents could spare time from farm repairs.

Kes, for one, couldn't bear the thought of not going back into the inner cavern. The twins were mad to explore the rest of the caves. Finn, always the most cautious of them all, agreed, but only if they all promised never to go in unless everyone was together, and then only if they did it properly with guide ropes, torches, back-up safety ropes and candles — everything he could think of.

'Sounds like a school excursion,' complained Jon.

'Don't come then.'

'OK. You don't have to yell at us.'

'That or nothing. Come on, get going; we're going to be late for Brian.'

'It won't ever happen, anyhow,' Sarah said. 'Jack's sure to tell, he's such a blabbermouth, and we'll be stopped.'

'You're the one who tells everyone everything,' Jack shouted. 'What about when you told Mai about Finn kissing that girl on the bus? Hey? The stupid-looking one with the Bali T-shirt. Yuk, how revolting.

That dumb whining Shelley kid who sounds like a horse. "Hello, Fiiiinny. Is anyone sitting here? Can I sit here, Fiiiinny?" As if Finny baby owns all the bus seats.'

Jack stuck his fingers down his throat, lost the plot, and forgot for once that he was arguing with Sarah.

Chapter 15

IT WAS NEARLY 11 o'clock when Brian arrived. The train was so delayed that he and Mai had had a meal in Moe before coming home. Angie insisted on staying up to welcome him, and Finn, since Brian was sleeping in his room, could hardly avoid it.

Angie had bullied then cajoled Finn into promising that he'd make Brian feel welcome. As they got ready for bed he kept trying, but Brian was so withdrawn he hardly answered him. Finn climbed into bed and went to sleep.

Brian lay awake for hours, staring at the stars slowly turning around the south celestial pole, trying to shake the fear that sometimes sat him upright. He saw the dawn break, heard the first noises of strange birds on the roof and fell asleep, exhausted.

Still tired out the next day, he lay on the veranda couch reading and talking to Angie who hadn't left his side and wouldn't let anyone else near him on their own. In the late afternoon she talked him into going for a ride on the horses. He admitted he was a useless rider, but Angie persevered, promising that if he could get a trot out of Freda he'd be unique. Eventually, Brian agreed and they rode out towards the billabong for the best part of two hours.

Finn and Kes were embarrassed; Angie was putting them to shame.

'I feel sorry for him,' Kes said to Finn, 'but my heart's not in it. It's still hard work talking to him. He doesn't offer much, does he? Still looks like he wouldn't give ten cents for the lot of us. Did you see his face when he came out this morning and looked around in the light? I think he feels he's in a war zone.'

'Well, he is. I don't know, Kes. He annoys the hell out of me, but he looks beaten up, doesn't he? Shrunk somehow. He's shorter than I remember and not as arrogant.'

'He didn't fall over himself with joy at the sight of us again. So much for talking about us all the time.'

'The myth and the reality.'

'Profound, Finn!'

'End of year exam question.'

It was Mai who decided enough was enough. After dinner, she called Angie inside to cut her hair, forcing the issue with the older two. Angie gave Brian up reluctantly, unspoken threats in the stares she aimed at her brother and cousin.

Kes and Finn sat with Brian on the Lawsons' veranda steps. The day had cooled to bearable and the cicadas were deafening. Kes's mind kept wandering back to the caves. It was boring talking to Brian, who only asked an occasional polite question then drifted off into his own thoughts before she could finish answering. All her conversations ran into dead ends. He seemed completely contained within himself.

'Aren't these cicadas incredible! They make my ears ring. They must've still been underground when the fire came through,' Kes said.

'The fire didn't have any effect on the flies, unfortunately,' said Finn, waving them away from his face. 'If anything, they're worse.'

'It must've been terrible.' Brian spoke so quietly Kes hardly heard him.

'What? The fire? Yes, it was,' said Kes, surprised that he'd mentioned it.

'And it could get worse,' said Finn.

'How d'you mean?' Brian turned a blank face.

'Well, look at it, man!' Finn snapped. 'Does it look like it can support two families? We're broke. We might have to leave. It's been bad enough with the drought. This is the final straw.'

Brian hugged his knees and stared at the rows of evening hills, each successive ridge a deeper shade of steel blue, each with a shimmering bronze edge. Like knives, he thought.

'It must've been terrible … and then … maybe you have to leave. I shouldn't be here,' he said distantly.

'No, it's all right,' Kes was quick to respond. 'We're glad you wanted to come. It must be horrible for you with your dad in hospital and not knowing what …' She trailed off awkwardly.

'Yes. Sorry,' Finn said. 'Sorry about the way I just spoke. It's been a disaster the past few weeks. We're pretty badly messed up and we're all edgy. Not much fun to be around.'

'I shouldn't have come. Mum shouldn't have asked. She knew you'd been burnt out, we saw it on TV. Saw footage of the Federation Valley and the plateau up here on fire. It was horrible — your place was still burning. The helicopter was hovering right overhead — I could pick out your two houses clearly.'

'I bet you could. They're the only things left standing.'

Kes glanced at Finn. Brian's mother had been caught out lying to Mai. Perhaps she was desperate; she'd be worried out of her mind about her husband.

'Mum said — Mum said she was glad the lovely antique furniture hadn't been burnt.'

'Now that was right nice of her,' Finn said sarcastically.

'… but Dad said the fire was probably the end of the line as far as the farm was concerned.'

Kes interrupted him before Finn let fly. 'Have your friends been good since your dad got crook?'

Brian looked at her and gave a half laugh. 'Oh yeah. Great.' Kes couldn't fathom him; didn't know what to make of that response.

'Andrew, my best friend, he's been OK. He

wanted me to stay with him, but Mum thought it'd be good for me to get right out of Melbourne. She's crazy. I just worry more about Dad when I can't see him. But thanks for inviting me, I didn't really want ... didn't really think you'd want to have me back,' he added awkwardly.

'Oh.' Kes thought frantically, and came up with nothing. 'Oh. That's OK. Glad you wanted to come. We'll try and do a bit better than last time, hey?' She grinned at his troubled face. 'We promise to improve our behaviour, don't we, Finn?' Kes kicked him.

'I really worry about Dad. I won't see him now until after his operation.'

'You can ring him,' Finn offered. 'The phone lines were burnt out, but the new mobile works.'

Finn stood up and saw Brian smile for the first time since he'd known him. 'You can talk to him now if you want. I'll tell Dad. They're home, early tonight for some reason.'

'Yeah? Thanks. That'd be great. The doctors keep saying he'll be all right. They say they've done this operation a hundred times before. They tried to make it sound like an appendectomy, but it's not. They're opening up his heart. That's bloody serious as far as I'm concerned. It might be a piece of piss to a heart surgeon, but it's my dad they're messing about with.'

Kes hesitated, remembering the man she had so loathed such a short time — such a lifetime — ago.

'They're really smart now. Mr Faulkner had four of his arteries replaced and his heart put in a bag or something, like you get around oranges. He's really fit now. Sorry. You probably don't want to hear that.'

'No, it's OK. No one'll talk to me about it, except one young doctor, an Asian bloke.' He glanced at Finn leaning over the step rail, 'They all talk to Mum and totally ignore me, as if I don't count, or don't care.' He added something under his breath that neither of them caught. 'You're lucky. Your parents talk to you. Mine fight,' he said to the sinking sun, as if the distance could absorb the painful words.

Kes put her arm around his shoulders. He winced under her touch and she casually removed it as if she hadn't noticed.

He was acutely aware of the presence of these two beside him. He could imagine that if they'd been friends they might be trying by their nearness to protect him, to prevent the blow he could feel ready to fall. They might stave off the inevitable, ward off things he couldn't bear to consider.

'They fight when they get under pressure,' Kes said. 'Ours do. Don't they, Finn? We hear them. Other people might think they're perfect, seeing them from the outside, but they're not. They're just ordinary; they get bad-tempered sometimes. Even Mai.'

'But Mai wouldn't …'

'Oh yes she would. Mai really cracks the shits when she loses it, doesn't she, Finn?'

Finn was looking down the track. 'Car's coming. Funny time for a visitor.' He shaded his eyes against the glare of the setting sun, 'Oh, it's only Hamish. Local cop,' he said to Brian.

'It's Dad! Something's happened to him!' Brian leapt up.

'Hang on!' Kes grabbed his shirt and pulled him down, 'Don't jump to such wild conclusions. Dad and Charlie are in the SES. Hamish coordinates this area. He often calls in on his way home.'

The police car pulled up in the yard and a young man in uniform got out. He lifted his hand to them, started in their direction, then changed his mind and headed for the kitchen door.

'It's Dad, I know it is.'

'They're deciding where and when to hold their next practice session, and what they'll do.'

'Three times he nearly died. They had to artificially revive him twice.'

'That's terrible! He was in hospital already?'

'Yes.' Brian stared at the kitchen door in silence. 'Just as well.'

Ten minutes passed. The twins rode past, chasing the dogs. A magpie with a burnt wing hopped up onto the veranda. Emma, foraging along the veranda baseboards, gave Brian a wide berth.

'She should be more grateful to you.' Kes smiled at him. 'She's the most spoilt bird in Victoria, probably Australia.' But Brian barely glanced at the emu.

Kes shouted at the twins not to ride over the piles of rubble — that they'd puncture their tyres.

The kitchen door opened and Charlie called them.

'I knew it.' Brian leapt up and ran down the veranda. 'What's happened to Dad?'

Mai, Charlie, Pat and Hamish sat around the table. Angie, her hair half-cut, looked shocked.

'What's happened to Dad?' Brian was shouting.

'Sit down, son … all of you. Your father's all right, Brian, nothing has changed. He's still due to be operated on tomorrow.'

Brian flopped down on a chair, searching their faces. An awkward silence went on too long. No one was looking at him, Angie was staring at her hands. Mai and Hamish started to speak together.

'It's your mother, Brian,' Mai said gently. 'She's been in a car accident.'

'No!' he shouted, as if it was not too late to prevent.

'It was a nasty one, but she'll be all right … after a while. There was a head-on collision and your mother has broken both her legs. She's all right apart from that, there's no other damage to her head or her body. Unfortunately, her legs took the full impact of the crash.'

'No! How? Where is she? I've gotta go!' He stood, looking around wildly. 'Where is she? Where did it happen? Oh, shit! Both of them now.'

Mai said, 'The accident happened this morning, right outside the hospital. Your mother had just dropped some things off there for your father and the car she was in was hit as it came out onto the road. It was spun around into oncoming traffic. A truck hit the passenger side, the front bonnet crumpled right in and her legs were crushed.'

Brian gasped and his face turned deathly pale. Mai reached across the table and took his hand. 'She's had them operated on already, and now one of them's in traction to make sure the bones knit straight. She'll have to stay in hospital, though, for as long as she's in traction.'

'Maybe you've got the wrong person. I mean she might have the same name ... or something ... but it's not my mother?' he appealed to Hamish like a little child.

Hamish said, 'I'm sorry, Brian. There's no mistake. I've just spoken to the sergeant who attended the accident. Your mother passed on the information to us about where to find you.'

Brian looked as if he'd been slapped. 'They can't both be in hospital. What'll I do? Who was she with? Who was driving the car?'

'A Mr Johnnie Pike,' Hamish replied. 'He has a broken nose, concussion and some smashed teeth.'

Brian's face turned crimson with rage. 'Good. Saves me doing it.'

Kes put her hand on Brian's shoulder but he flung it off and buried his head in his hands.

'When's she coming out of hospital?'

'Not for six or seven weeks, maybe eight,' Mai replied.

'Eight weeks!' He lifted his angry face. 'But what about Dad? How'll I look after him? I don't know what to do.'

'He'll be in hospital for a couple of weeks, but when he's well enough to come out, you'll get a lot of help; nurses who'll visit every day, home help, transport assistance. You two'll have a lot of support.'

Kes rushed in. 'You'll stay with us now though, won't you, Brian? I mean, if you want to — can't he, Mai? If you'd like to, rather than going straight back to Melbourne?'

'Brian's welcome to stay here as long as he wants, but probably he has friends or relatives that he'd rather be with at this time.' Mai smiled at his tear-stained face. 'But we'd like you to stay with us, for a few days at least. Unless you want to go straight away.'

'I wouldn't know where to go.'

'You don't have to go anywhere. You're here and we want you to stay if you'd like to,' Mai repeated.

'We don't see any of our relatives. Mum hates Dad's family and Dad hates Mum's. There wouldn't be anywhere to stay. It'll be worse now — everyone'll be running away as fast as they can. I never should've come. You probably never even invited me in the first place, did you? Mum said you had, but she manipulates everyone, you can't trust anything she says.'

Charlie started to reply, but Brian wasn't listening. Kes was lost in the sadness of Brian's world. She couldn't imagine having no friends or family that she could run to when she was in this much need. Finn was no help; he was sitting with his mouth hanging open.

Angie, still with half a haircut, disappeared to find Sarah. They had hardly seen each other all day. Angie needed Sarah and Sarah was jealous of Brian.

Brian rang both his father and his mother. He said little about the calls, but was shocked by his parents' total lack of concern about each other. 'They sound as if they're already divorced,' Kes heard him say to Mai. 'Dad said the accident was her own fault. It wouldn't have happened if she hadn't been out with Johnnie. Mum said it was Dad's fault, it wouldn't have happened if she hadn't been running around after him. Neither of them asked me how the other one was. I don't think they remembered. It was that unimportant.'

At Mai's suggestion, Kes and Finn took Brian for a walk. It was already dark, but the intense heat of the day had faded with the light. The three of them went cross-country in the direction of Federation and picked up the track that ran to the edge of the plateau, where Kes had driven Brian two months before. Finn and Kes flanked Brian who, unaware of where he was, stumbled along in the dark between them.

From the house, the track wound for kilometres through the black maze of burnt-out scrub before emerging abruptly at the cliff edge. There was a look-out point here, where the old miners' track dropped sharply down into Federation.

His mother's accident had shocked Brian deeply. That she'd been with Johnnie Pike, whom he hated, was the final straw.

It seemed to Kes and Finn that he'd been pushed beyond his capacity.

As they walked, Brian's furious monologue hardly halted, veering wildly between raging independence and tearful self-pity. Anger and betrayal spilled out of him in a frightened, unstoppable flood. He spoke rapidly, furiously, as a lifetime of hurt welled up and poured out. For almost the whole hour it took to reach the rim of the plateau, the other two heard revelations that they knew he'd regret the next day, but there was no stopping or distracting him. When he finally stopped speaking, the night was strangely quiet.

They'd reached the edge of the plateau. Kes loved this lookout point by day or by night, but it seemed as if a pall of sadness and anger now hung over it. Down the track, there was a sudden scrabble in the bushes and a faint cry. Some animal had just made a kill.

It was becoming brighter, with a great floodlight of a full moon rising behind the burnt skeletons of forest giants. Since the fire, the normal activity of the nocturnal creatures was gone, it was almost silent at night now. Kes jumped as a powerful owl swept across their heads. Only the hunters and the carrion-eaters fared well these days.

Beyond the massive grey boulders where they now sat, the track dropped steeply. The way down the spur was impassable, blocked with fallen timber.

'There's supposed to be the ghost of a miner who lived on this track. Piper's ghost,' Kes told Brian, 'the old prospector that the mine's named after. The place I took you to, remember? People say he drives his pair of bullocks up here through all these fallen trunks. No one I know's ever seen him though,' Kes added.

The few streetlights of Federation, keyholes in the darkness below them, outlined the main street and Gloriana Creek several kilometres away. A single car drove through Federation and branched off to the right at the top of the town.

Finn pointed to the spur road. 'That's our road, the one that comes up to this plateau. That'll be the McLarens coming home. It's only them and us on this road.'

The lights of the town flickered and went out as they watched, and the Gloriana Creek valley suddenly became indistinguishable from the surrounding blackness.

'What happened?'

'The generator goes off at eleven,' Finn replied. 'There's no mains electricity in the town, although it's coming in next year. Most of the locals don't want to go on the grid though, they're on bottled gas and solar power.'

'So easy. Flick a switch and go out.'

'Brian!'

'It would be. No more shit.'

'Your father needs you,' it was the first thing that came into Kes' head, 'so does your mother.'

'Yeah.'

'You can't tell what's going to happen when they both come out of hospital,' Finn said. 'Things could be different — better. They'll have had a long time to think about stuff, including you.'

'Yeah.' Brian slid off the boulder and turned away from the plateau edge, heading back along the track.

Kes wondered if he could leave his damaging childhood behind. If he'd ever grow to be strong and gentle like her father. Brian's problems seemed so small compared with the life her father had led by his age. She watched him stomping down the track ahead of them, his hands jammed in his pockets. His mouth was clamped shut, as if he couldn't bear to speak again. Kes wondered if he could develop the strength he'd need.

Brian seemed to read her mind. He stopped and turned around to face them. The moon was directly behind him and the other two were illuminated brightly against the black of the forest. He looked at them for a long minute. Kes's gentle dark face smiled back at him, Finn's golden skin shone in the moonlight. Two months ago he'd felt only disdain for them, hadn't wanted their company. He had thought himself superior and wished himself a hundred ks away from them, this idealised family of Angie's that had died in the meeting. Now, more than anything, he craved their friendship.

'I know you didn't invite me. Don't go on pretending you did. I don't know why Mum did it, but she did, probably to get rid of me so she could spend more time with precious Johnnie.' His voice sounded lonely as a child's. 'I don't want to pretend anything ever again. I'm sick to death of it, living in this cage of lies. It's a rat-trap. I thought once, before I met you, that you could maybe be my friends. Angie used to spend hours talking about you in hospital. You were like an imaginary family that I had inside my head.

'I think I've remembered everything Angie ever said about you. You'll think I'm mad, but Angie was — is — the closest thing I'll ever have to a little sister.'

Finn felt a prick of jealousy. Angie was his little sister; he wasn't ready to share her, especially not with Brian.

'That's how I started thinking about you as this imaginary family. Crazy, hey? You've probably no idea how much I know about all of you, from when you were kids. I even know stuff like how you pushed Kes out of a tree, Finn, and broke her arm when she was six, and how Sarah and Angie dug under the foundations of your house to make a cubby. I know you want to be a vet, and Kes is so good at biology she'll be an ornithologist. I know how the twins painted a dog red at their kindergarten, and how the primary school asked your mum to take them home after their first week when they dismantled the airconditioning under the portable. I heard how Jack ran the tractor into the dam and tried to blame a telephone technician. I know tons of stuff about you. Angie and I used to talk for hours and sometimes she'd have a few of the nurses there as well, all listening to her stories. She's a great storyteller.

'Then when I met you, it was such a shock! You weren't anything like I'd thought. I knew you loathed me from the start. It was such a horrible weekend!' He wiped his face, 'My parents fighting, screaming at each other, from Melbourne to Moe. Mum making up lies so she could dump me on you, then me getting lost and taking that emu egg, thinking you'd be impressed. All the time knowing you thought I was a fake.'

Finn said, 'I don't think we helped much. In fact, I'm sure we didn't ...'

'The fantasy family that turned out to be an illusion. What a surprise!' Brian sounded bitter.

'... but we don't have to keep on that way,' Finn continued. 'We're not as bad as you think.'

'It's not you that worry me. It's me. How am I going to break free of all this? I've lived like this all my life, in such a big web of lies, it feels normal. If you want something you invent some story to get your own way. It's the way our family operates.'

'You aren't tied by the leg to past things ... even

if they hurt like hell. Anyway, you can still fly with one leg,' Finn said.

'You can't let it strangle you. You *can* get away from your childhood, I know you can.' Kes thought of the small child being lifted up and taken from his parents. She breathed deeply and tried to put it out of her mind.

Finn thought of the great wall of fire rolling down on top of them, felt Kes's hand slip from his, and his frantic grab for her. The sweat started in his palms, and he wondered who he was trying to kid.

They were both silent. Brian stole a glance at them, wondering what they were thinking, why they looked so absent and whether he'd completely alienated them with this final outburst. It had sounded so self-pitying.

'Anyhow, that's what I'm doing from now on. No more crap. No more living in the baited trap. No more pretence, from my parents or me. That's enough. Finished. So why don't you tell me about the cave?' he added, with one of his rare smiles.

Kes and Finn were shocked. 'Who told you? Oh, of course, Angie, yesterday, when you rode out to the waterhole.'

'She didn't mean to, she slipped up.'

'It's OK. It's just that we haven't told our parents. They'll worry themselves sick about it. It'd be enough to make one of them give up work, and we can't afford that, so just keep it to yourself.'

'I suppose if you know about it, you can see it,' Finn said. 'We'll show you after the weekend. Our mums'll be home tomorrow, it's Saturday. We can't risk going in there when they're home. We'll be caught, sure as.'

Kes said. 'You will stay, won't you? Please, Brian.'

'If you can put up with me.'

'Good. That's sorted.'

Chapter 16

Brian's father had been operated on and was in intensive care. His mother was mending, but still in a lot of pain. On short notice, Kate and Mai had to go to the families' solicitor in Melbourne. They were leaving Monday and said they'd take Brian with them to visit his parents.

The kids had been given an hour free before lunch, to go down to the waterhole and cool off.

Brian sat in the water, then wandered off after Angie and Sarah. Despite their conversation on their long walk, Kes still felt inadequate to deal with him. She had no experience of growing up in a fighting, hostile family, and was always afraid of saying the wrong thing, or that she wouldn't be able to hide her dislike of both his parents.

Kes kept staring up the valley that hid the cave entrance. She couldn't forget the painted walls and the feeling that the spirits of the people still lived on in the caves. Last night, for the first time in ages, she hadn't dreamt of either the fire or of her father, but of the spirit person who looked at her with wide white eyes and spoke words that she couldn't understand.

Kes decided that when they told their parents about the cave, she'd ask Rose Bannock to visit and tell her about the handprints and the painted man. She knew they were important, very important. No prints and no painted figure like this had ever been found in Gippsland, as far as she could discover, none closer than the Grampians in the east of the state, hundreds of kilometres away.

She wondered how Rose was going tracing her dad's family. So much had happened since then — the fire, the cave — it all seemed like a year ago, though it was only two months.

The twins had decided that since gold was heavy, it might have washed out of the hills and settled in the deepest part of the lagoon. They were dredging up buckets of sand from the bottom, arguing about whether it was more likely to be at one end or the other. They broke the bucket fighting over it, and went on fighting for the fun of it.

Angie and Sarah had left the slopes and were out on the swamp, teaching Brian to track.

Finn thrashed up and down the length of the billabong. He wanted to be out on the fences with Pat and Charlie. Their mothers were both home to help Kes if she needed it. He was experienced in fencing work. He'd been working with his father since he was young, rounding up cattle on his own since he was the twins' age. He was nine when he first learned to ride a motorbike on the hills, and ten when he worked on his first muster up in the ranges. He was thin and slight, a beanpole who looked as if a puff of wind would knock him over, but he was all wire. He smiled to himself. 'Marshmallow covered wire,' Kes called him.

He got out of the water and glanced over at her. She was staring at the mountains again. What was the matter with her these days? It was as if she'd begun a slow unstoppable drift away from him. He couldn't remember when it had started. Before the fire; if anything that had brought her back for a while.

A few days ago they had talked about the fire for the first time in ages, about running down the hill to the dugout. Kes couldn't remember it. She said she remembered feeling his hand pulling her, a roaring wall of flame at their backs, but that they were flying, not running.

Where did she go lately, with that closed face and stubborn look? Sometimes she didn't talk to him for days on end and he missed her hugely.

He edged over to her. She was hunched up at the edge of the water drawing patterns in the sand. Blinds down. No one at home.

She turned to him suddenly, her eyes wide and startled. 'What's it like to be Chinese?' she said, without preamble.

That was the last thing he'd expected. 'Geez, Kes! I don't know. I don't ever think about it.'

'Why not? You should. Why don't you? How can you avoid thinking about it?'

'For Christ's sake, Kes! Where did this come from? How the hell should I know what it's like? I just am. A bit yellow, straight black hair, eyes that go up a bit. I don't spend all day looking at myself in the mirror, wondering what half's what. Like that bloody awful joke Dad still insists on telling — that Angie and I are half white and half Wong.'

'Don't be stupid. I ask you a serious question and you joke. You always joke about things.'

'Hang on! You don't need to shout at me — and don't be so aggro! Why should I think about it? It doesn't bother me? It doesn't bother Angie, or Gill to be half Greek for that matter.'

'No! I want to know about *you*. Don't avoid the issue.'

'So! It's an "issue", is it? It must be serious!'

'Well?'

'Well, what? Where do you want me to start? When I was a little kid sensitive about being different and I punched up Tommy Toghill in Year 3 for calling me a chink and a slope?'

'Yes. Start there.'

'We fought, he belted me up, and when we were called inside he couldn't remember why we were fighting. I did, and said he started it, but he said I started it, so we both copped it and spent the lunch hour sitting at our desks. You want me to go on?'

'Yes.'

'That afternoon on the bus home we had another fight and Mr Maddocks put us off and drove around the corner. We were so scared we'd have to walk the sixty ks home, we sorted it out and lived happily ever after. Tom's a good mate, but he still reckons I started it.'

'Your mum says you have a rich Chinese culture behind you.'

'Yeah, well, that's Mum. If you're interested in that stuff. She is, but she's been there a few times. China's as foreign to me as Africa. Sure, they look a bit like me, but do they think like me? How much do the Chinese know about cattle farming in the Baw Baws, and how much do I know about the Ming dynasty? They made vases, that's about all I know. I don't even like them, all those weird mountains, pink dragons and weeping willow stuff. I like herefords and gum trees. I like living here. I don't like bushfires, and I don't like you disappearing off into the back of your brain space and shutting the door on me.'

'I don't! I've never done that!'

'You do. You do it all the time lately. You were doing it just then when I came over. I spoke to you twice before you answered me.'

'I didn't hear you. You didn't.'

'Don't look at me like that, you stubborn mule. I did.'

'I must be going mad.' Kes drew circles in the sand. 'It's the cave, Finn … seeing the hands on the walls and the fires on the floor. It's really stirred up something in me. I keep wondering who I am.'

'It started before we found the cave.'

There was a long silence while they both stared at the twins trying to drown each other.

'Jon, let him breathe,' Kes called out automatically.

'You know when it started? Before the fire. Before the end of school. The first time was coming home on the bus, that day you got so mad with me. I was talking to Shelley and I turned around and said something to you. You stared at me like I was a real creep, then tore shreds off me for making some silly remark. I thought you'd suddenly got mad because I was talking to her while I was going out with Gill. Or jealous of me because of Gill or some other bloody thing. I didn't know. You certainly wouldn't tell me.'

'Jealous of Gill? Don't be daft. She's my best friend — after you. She's smart and she's real. How could I be jealous of her? That's a dumb thing to think. Really dumb. Anyhow, why didn't you ask me? I'm not a mind-reader, you know.'

The injustice of this remark even struck Kes. She laughed and put out her hand to him. 'I'm sorry, Finn. You're my best mate. Look, I'm doing something and I don't even know whether or not it's "ethical", to use your favourite word.' She paused. 'And if you say it *is* unethical, I'll scream.'

'Go on. It sounds dicey. If I'm your best mate, you'd better tell me before you get in up to your ears.'

'I'm in it already, over my head. I'm trying to find Dad's family.'

'Jesus! Kes! Does he know?'

'No.'

'Do you think he wants you to? I mean, what if they don't want to know about him? What if they abandoned him and forgot about him?'

'I don't believe that.'

'Why not? It happens. You mean, you don't want to believe it. How do you know? Families do abandon kids, you can't ignore that. They've never tried to find him. They've had plenty of time to do that, it's not like last century. There are records kept of people. They don't just come unlabelled.'

'He was taken away from his family when he was two.'

'Or they gave him away.'

'Then he ran away from the Wangaratta farm when he was fifteen and he didn't want to be found.'

'What makes you think he does now?'

'I don't know. Don't look at me like that, Finn, you're supposed to be helping. That's my problem! Is it right, what I'm doing? And if I find out about them and they're horrible or they don't want to know about him, what do I do with that? Do I tell him? "Found your family, Dad, they're real creeps and they don't want to know you." Or do I keep the information about his birth family, secret from my own father?'

'Then why did you start, for Christ's sake? You've got yourself into something you can't handle.'

'Thanks, friend. I really needed to be told I was a dickhead.'

'Sorry. I can't think of the answers either.'

'I started because one day out on the swamp Sarah asked him to teach her how to track and got angry with him when he didn't know anything about tracking or his family. She shouted at him that he wasn't an emu, he couldn't just lose his family like Emma.'

'Ever tactful Sarah. If you think it, say it.'

'Well, at least she's clear and definite. She never gets into bloody knots about things like I do.'

'No, and watch out anyone within spitting distance. Stand clear, here comes Sarah sailing under a full head of steam! Go on about Pat: what then?'

'Dad stared at the mountains and he looked so sad I thought he'd cry, and he said he wouldn't let past wrongs ruin his happiness now.'

'I see.'

'You don't! You had to be there and see his eyes. He also said he'd wished many times that he knew his family, where he'd come from. That's what started it. After I talked to Rose Bannock.'

'Who?'

'The community education person from the

Aboriginal Co-op in the Valley. That was the day I was snaky to you on the bus. After that day it became important for me, too, that I knew who I was and where I'd come from. They're my grandparents too, Finn. Don't you understand? You know yours, I don't know a single other person from that side of my family. The people I get my skin colour and God knows what else from. I want to find them for me as well.'

'Then at least be clear what you're doing it for. Is it for you or Pat or both?'

'For both of us, I think … and for Sarah and the twins, they have a right to know, too.'

'Yeah, well, I don't know where everyone's rights start and finish in this. Leave the little kids out of it for a minute. Who has the greater right, you or Pat?'

'I don't know. That's why I'm trying to talk to you.' She stared miserably at the twins. 'Jack! For God's sake, give him a break. Jon, get away from him. Grow up, can't you! No, don't,' she added, under her breath, 'it's no fun.'

She yelled at Jack again who took no notice and went on dunking Jon. She jumped up and ran down into the water.

Finn watched her. It was a brave thing to start … or dumb. Depending on how it turned out. She'd win or lose this one with a bang. He hadn't been much help, it was such a shock — the last thing he'd expected. He'd try again when she got out.

It was more than tracing her grandparents

though. She'd started the conversation by asking him what it was like to be Chinese. It was very close, personal, more about finding her Aboriginal roots. 'I keep wondering who I am,' she'd said. My grandparents were Scottish and Chinese, that's what I am, Finn thought, watching Kes trying to separate the twins, and I couldn't care less — or maybe I do more than I think. But I don't have Kes's problem ... or do I and I just haven't worried about it the way she has? Maybe it's something that Australian Chinese worked out in the days of mining and market gardens, and I take advantage of their battles and don't have to think about it. Isn't that what every generation does? Takes what the older one wins for them as their right and never says thank you. Isn't that what the old soldiers were always on about, how they'd made the world free for their kids who didn't appreciate it?

Finn didn't know anything about the First and Second World Wars except old codgers marching on Anzac Day, and a lot of stuff about young men giving their life for their country. It was ancient history, as far as he was concerned, as ancient as the Peloponnesian wars. But the Aboriginal people were going through tough times now. It was raw. Old wounds being heard for the first time by a generation of whites who found them hard to believe and come to terms with.

Finn watched Kes yelling at Jack to get off his brother. Is that what was chewing her up as well? Wik? Land rights? The stolen generation? Christ! That might be Pat. His uncle. Not some unknown person on TV who you felt bad about, then forgot too soon. The loving, gentle uncle who was his second father. It was that close to home.

Finn kicked at the sand. Pat, a stolen child? A two-year-old baby taken from his home? What about Pat's parents, had they run after the truck that took away their son? Like that father who followed a truck for three days. Jesus Christ, how could he be so bloody thick and stupid? It could've been Pat on that truck or one of a thousand children like him.

A wave of anger rippled through him. He turned and looked at Kes wading in the water, breaking up the stranglehold Jon had on Jack's neck. She was years ahead of him in understanding, he felt a real idiot.

She turned and looked at him as if she'd heard every thought racing through his mind. He nodded at her. She smiled back, understanding.

Chapter 17

IN THE FARM office, on Sunday morning, Angie and Sarah watched Mai sorting piles of papers. Mai and Kate were driving to Melbourne the next day for appointments with their insurance agent, the bank and the solicitor. They'd take Brian to visit his parents, then stay at least one night in town.

'If you're all going to be in Melbourne, can we camp down at the billabong, Mum?'

Mai stood up and went to the filing cabinet. She was only half listening. 'Yes. I suppose so. What?'

'Can we camp down by the billabong while you're in Melbourne? It's great down there.' Sarah shuffled the piles of paper.

'Yes. I don't know. Don't mess that stuff up, Sarah. Kes and Finn will have to agree. It'd be up to them. And your fathers.'

'They're never home till ten o'clock at night. You know Dad's useless,' said Angie. 'He says hello and goes to bed. He's gone by the time I wake up.'

'Yeah. My dad's the same. They won't care. So can we?'

'They will care if they have to come by the water-hole on their way home to check up on you. They do care anyhow, Sarah! Angie! How can you think such a thing! They're just over their heads in work right now.'

'Mum! Get real!' said Angie. 'We spend all day at the waterhole. Why on earth do you think we need to be checked up on? In case the bunyip gets us? In case of the monster that crawls from the swamp? The twins are our best defence, no monster in its right mind would come near them — twin monsters from the great white house on the hill.'

Mai laughed. 'It's fine with me. Sarah hold these, will you? Why can't I find that other insurance policy? I checked all this stuff after the fire. I had it then.'

'There's something stuck up behind the clock in the living room,' said Angie.

'That's right! Thanks. I put it there specially so it wouldn't get lost. Angie, do you know if Brian's packed an overnight bag yet? Does he need anything washed?'

'Yes, he has. No, he doesn't. So can we?'

'Can you what?'

'Mum! Keep your mind on what I'm saying! Can we camp at the billabong until you get back?'

'Camp? No! Oh yes, I suppose so, I can't really imagine you getting into much trouble down there. OK, now where's the deed to the other house?'

'On top of the fridge.'

'Why aren't they together? Honestly, I must be losing my marbles. Yes, I guess you can, anyhow Kes'll have the ute. Kes and Finn can get you back to the house in half an hour if they have to.'

'Good. We're going then.'

'Ask Kate first. Only if she agrees. And tell Kes and Finn I want to talk to them,' Mai shouted at their backs as they disappeared outside.

As far as the twins were concerned, there wasn't much else but gold in their lives. They still had gold fever running at a constant forty degrees Centigrade. They'd decided, last night in their tent, that there definitely would be gold in the bottom of the waterhole, and they'd dredge it out.

'One nugget per bucket,' they told Finn seriously, 'even if they're small.'

Finn insisted that they mine at the far end, complaining that the water was getting like a cattle dam where they'd churned it up.

It was nine o'clock in the morning; Pat and Charlie had just left the waterhole for the fences. Despite the fact that they said they wouldn't, their fathers had come to check on them last night on their way home, and again this morning on the way out to the ranges, 'Just in case.'

The twins were urging everyone to get breakfast. Kes had promised them pancakes. They were starving, they said, and wanted to get on with their dredging. The three girls wanted to go back to the cave.

The twins said there wasn't any gold in caves and they'd go caving after they found a nugget, which wouldn't take long.

'When hell freezes over,' Sarah said.

By the end of breakfast, they'd compromised enough to spend the rest of the morning around the waterhole and the afternoon exploring and mapping the cave.

Sarah and Angie went off to see what activity had taken place on the swamp. The dunnart had been eating well, the shells of dead beetles marked the entrance to its tiny grass nest hidden in a hollow log. A snake had been hunting past the entrance, too, perhaps hoping that it might be unwary.

Several wombats had been active on the far edge, and in one spot it looked as if there had been a fight. A piece of fur lay on the clay, and the surface was broken with angry-looking claw marks. The signs of a fresh rabbit kill lay near the fox's customary hideout. On the far side, the emus and roos were grazing together on the sedges that still grew on the swamp edge. The fire had missed most of the swamp — the fleshy succulents around the edge that the roos loved would not burn and the dried-out centre was cracked dolomite clay on which nothing ever grew.

'Dad and Pat must've been really late last night.'

'They didn't come past until after ten, Finn and Kes were still up talking,' said Sarah. 'You were already asleep. I was watching the stars and trying to stay awake. The Southern Cross turns in a great arc over the house hill.'

'The fence is almost finished in that section of the ranges paddock, you know,' said Angie. 'They've reached the back corner. Dad said there are still a few big pockets of scrub that the fire missed and we might be able to put a few cattle back in there. If we can afford the stock, that is.'

The roos, startled, sat up and watched the two figures approaching. A couple of emus, perhaps Emma's siblings, took fright and ran across the claypan, zigzagging as if the girls were chasing them, their bottoms flopping up and down as they ran.

It was getting close to noon. The sun was almost directly overhead and the claypan was baking. Even the deep imprints of the emus from the last spring rains cast no shadows.

Sarah sighed. 'What's going to happen to us, Angie? Do you reckon we're going to be able to stay here? I hear bits and pieces but I don't understand it all.'

'I know we're in deep trouble,' Angie replied. 'The loan from the bank is blowing out. That's the main reason why Mum and Kate had to go up to Melbourne yesterday. That and the insurance claim for the fire … apart from taking Brian. Mum was talking to Kate the night before they left. She'd forgotten I was there, I think. She said if things don't turn around soon, we might as well walk away. She looked terribly sad. It was after the weather report. The weather bloke had just said there was no end in sight to the drought, and that Gippsland was in crisis. He said it was the worst drought since 1886, the driest ten months on record.'

'You don't think we'll have to leave, do you? Do you, Angie? Like really go — sell the place? We can't. It's — it's us. We belong to it. Can you imagine not being here? I won't leave; I'm not walking away from here.' Panic rose in her voice, 'I'll run away. I'll go and live in the cave. Living in some shitty little dump in town where you can only take three steps before you hit the side fence. Can you imagine that?' She sat down on the baking clay, her eyes filling with tears that ran down her face and dripped off her chin. 'Walled in by paling fences. It'd be like prison, and we'd never get two houses together again. You'd all be somewhere, and we'd all be somewhere else, maybe even in a different town. We'd never be one family again.'

Angie swallowed and fought down the tears. She put her arms around Sarah. 'Something will come up. The luck of the Lawsons. People in Federation still talk about it, from the time old Ernest James found the first water in the hidden spring down in the back paddock. They called it liquid gold then. Look at the way the houses didn't burn down. And how Finn and Kate and Kes were safe in the fire.'

Sarah sniffed. 'You've got the craziest idea of luck, Angie. See that? Three hundred and sixty degrees. What isn't burnt to charcoal is dead. You're mad, Ang, but you're the best cousin.'

'They've got to talk to us though. It's worse not knowing. I wish they wouldn't try to hide things from us, like we were babies.'

'When they get back from Melbourne I'm going to ask them straight out if we'll have to leave,' said Sarah. 'It can't be any worse than what I'm imagining. Then I'll start planning, because I'm not leaving. Look for me in the cave if you have to. I'll find a place to hide in there that no one will ever find. I won't go. I WON'T GO! DO YOU HEAR ME? I'M NOT LEAVING!' she shouted at the hills.

In the afternoon they went caving. Kes and Finn put rope and torches, notebooks, pens and candles into the backpacks. The twins were carving great chunks of bread and meat into plate-sized sandwiches.

'OK, everyone,' said Finn, when they finally stood outside the cave. 'You know what we decided. We stay together. No one goes off exploring. No one plays silly buggers. That means you two, Jon and Jack. Don't lose sight of each other.'

'No, Finn.'

'Don't mess around. I'm serious. What we're doing's dangerous if we make mistakes.'

'Yes, Finn.'

'Do as teacher says,' said Jack.

Finn swatted him over the head. 'I'm not joking.'

'No, Mrs Singer.'

'You can bloody well stay out if you're going to bugger around,' he said angrily. 'Go back to the water-hole and play in the water if I can't trust you.'

'Aaaw, come on, Finn, we're just kidding.'

'Don't. I'm sick of the pair of you today.'

'Ooooo, Finn's in a bad mood.'

'Shut up, you two,' said Kes. 'Finn's right. It's dangerous or it could be if we go rushing around in there. If there are tunnels, there can be holes — remember that.'

'We'll map the caves,' Finn went on. 'Each have a go at it, then we'll come out and put them all together. We'll get one map that's accurate, that we all agree on.'

'Sounds like school,' grumbled Jon quietly to Jack, 'and he sounds like old Squawker Singer.'

Jack agreed, 'Yeah. Check with each other so you'll know if you're still breathing. You might've got lucky and died while I was boring you to death. Nag, nag, bloody nag.'

Jon thought that was incredibly funny.

Finn glared at him. 'Then we'll go a bit further, add a bit more, so we know exactly where we are all the time. We can go deeper, but not until we know what's behind us.'

They moved the packs inside the entrance. The sunlight shone feebly inside the cave, but the exit was a brilliant slit of sun against the rock walls. In the light of the seven torches, the cavern looked magical.

The first area was easy to map, simply the entrance cave and the one passage leading deeper into the side of the hill. They moved confidently along the passage they already knew towards the inner cave, branching off down the left-hand passage. They mapped the junction of the two passages and the second bigger cave, marking its entrances to the three unexplored passages and the five openings like port-holes, way above their heads.

Angie watched Sarah staring up at the holes. She suddenly knew that that was where she'd go to hide, and felt sick at the thought. She'd be terrified in there by herself, and too stubborn to leave. Sarah, turning, caught her look and turned away guiltily. Angie followed her miserably back to the first cavern where Finn wanted to compare their drawings in daylight.

The maps looked similar.

Kes was pleased, 'Jon's is really good. Somehow he's got it looking three-dimensional as well as it being a map.'

Finn spread the sketches out, discussing the next passage and how they'd draw the curving tubes. 'You ready?' he asked, leading them back into the entrance. 'Let's go.'

They wound along the passage, familiar now, branching off into the right-hand tunnel, trying to map all the twists and turns as they went. It was hard enough outside, let alone in a cramped, dark pipe, where you rapidly lost all sense of direction.

Kes was breathing quickly. Even though she knew what she'd see, the cave of handprints shocked her just as much as the first time. The roof was magnificent, the stronger lights bouncing flashes of light off the shining surfaces of the rocky stalactites.

Glowering at the six people who stood silent across the cave, was the watching figure of the black and white spirit man.

'That bloke gives me the creeps,' said Jack.

Jon agreed. 'Looks like he'd knock your head off and play footy with it.'

'Looks like Finn,' Jack said, muffling a laugh.

'I don't think we're supposed to be here,' said Kes, almost to herself.

'We're all right,' answered Finn. 'Nothing in here will come to any harm from us. You know that, and there's nothing here that can hurt us. Look around you, Kes.'

He looked at her worried face. 'Kes! You're scaring yourself. Get a grip. They're painted images, handprints on rock walls. Probably hundreds or thousands of years old.'

Kes shook herself and bent her head over her paper. This cave was easy to map. A long oval floor with just one other exit, the passage on the far side, guarded by the spirit person.

Kes took a deep breath and looked at the others.

They were watching her. 'You want to go on further?' she asked.

'I suppose so,' Sarah replied uncertainly, 'if you do.'

'We do,' said the twins.

Finn said, 'It's OK, Kes. It's a bit eerie, but it's safe. How about you lead? Then you can stop whenever you want. If it really gets to you, we'll go out and come back again later on.'

'Aaaw, no, Finn! Come on, Kes,' Jack groaned. 'We can't leave now. It's just getting really exciting. Get a life, Kes. Come on. Sarah'll hold your hand.'

'Shut up, you two,' said Sarah savagely.

Finn turned on them. 'Right, that's it. I've had it with you. You're out, right now. We all are.'

'Hang on, Finn. I'm OK. We can go on,' Kes broke in, 'but let's go now, before I lose my nerve. Really. I'm all right. It's just being so far underground, I think.'

'One more word out of you, Jack, and you're out.'

'Yes. Shut up, Jack,' said Sarah. 'You're a pain in the bum.'

Jack nodded, mimicking Finn as soon as he turned away. 'One more word out of you, Jack, and you're out. Crapologist.' Finn ignored him.

'What's the matter with him, anyway?' Jack complained quietly to Jon. 'He's fifteen. He thinks he's King Dick. He's just a plain big dick.'

'They all go crazy at fifteen. They start at fourteen and go on getting worse until they leave home.
Mum said so, I heard her.'

'Sarah'll be fifteen in a couple of years. She'll be
the worst. How do you reckon she does that stuff?'

'What, see all those things in the dirt?'

'No, that stuff with her eyes — make them zap at
you like that. Like you're standing in front of a pair of
stun guns. I swear I'm leaving home when Snake-Eyes
turns fifteen.'

'Let's go,' said Kes.

Silently, one behind the other, they passed
beneath the white-eyed figure and into the unexplored
passage.

Chapter 18

THE TUNNEL TWISTED and turned like the others. It, too, was smooth on the walls, cool and dry to touch, the floor sloping steadily and steeply downhill. They walked in single file behind Kes, not speaking, apprehensive at being in a new part of the cave again. Although they all had torches and the tunnel was a blaze of light, they had all caught a bit of Kes's anxiety.

The tunnel seemed to go on forever, all the time descending deeper into the bedrock. Sometimes it narrowed to a squeeze only just passable, sometimes it dropped to crawling height. After thirteen minutes, by Finn's watch, from the last cave it widened, allowing them to walk three abreast, but then the ceiling dropped again until they had to crouch, then crawl along a tube no bigger than a stormwater drain.

A few minutes further on, just as they thought they'd have to crawl out backwards and give up, the squeeze lifted to head level and a branching tunnel led off to the left. They could see it ending abruptly, after a few metres, in a fallen rock pile, where the roof had collapsed.

The smooth floor of the main tunnel now gave out into a broken mess of boulders and, for the first time, they hit mud, making it difficult to walk without slipping on the chopped surfaces. The tunnel climbed sharply, widened, then stopped, buried under a mass of broken rock that had tumbled out of the wall, almost blocking the way. The rock fall had left a gaping hole in the tunnel wall. From the top of the pile of fallen rock, they could see through into another whole series of spaces and tunnels. The ancient avalanche had created a window into another adjoining cave system.

'The whole hill must be a honeycomb,' Finn said.

'Pretty scary,' Angie said. 'I hope everyone remembers exactly where we've come from.'

They sat on the top of the rock pile, their heads touching the roof, drawing in details on the maps and considering what to do. Beyond the rock fall, the tunnel broke up a series of jagged cavities and high caves created by fracturing and faulting in the rock. There had been some major instability here at some time in the past. Fallen sheets of rock heeled over at wild angles, many of them unsupported, resting against walls and rock piles. They looked as if a push could send them crashing. There were no real roofs in any of these caves, just jagged extensions of the walls, deeply slashed into the solid rock above them.

'Do we go on?' Kes asked Finn.

'A metre at a time and very, *very* carefully.'

They crept forward slowly, testing each step. Above their heads, massive sheets of rock hung down into the cavern where they stood, searching for a way through the maze.

To their left, where an entire wall had collapsed in a gigantic shambles of rock, they found a small fissure. Squeezing through it, ankle-deep in mud, they found what looked like the extension of the original tunnel. It seemed, at first, to be blocked by two gigantic slabs of rock that had sheared off the roof, but the fall was stable and they could just slide under them.

The tunnel continued sloping down, widening and then narrowing, smooth again underfoot, with the same curved, water-carved tubular walls.

'It feels as if we're being buried in the intestines of the earth.' Finn's voice echoed along the passage.

'I don't think that's a very helpful remark,' Sarah replied. After that no one spoke.

They had walked about three or four hundred metres from the painted cave when Kes, in the lead, stopped them.

'Sssh! Stand still. I can hear something!' Everyone stopped breathing.

'It sounds like – water – I think,' Kes said finally.

'I thought you meant … something … else,' said Sarah, her voice quivering.

'Come on, Sarah! You're OK.' Finn laughed. 'Jack and Jon are by far the worst "Something Else" that you'll find around here.'

'Funny. Funny. Ha, ha, ha. Least we aren't wetting our pants like you guys, worrying if the earth's eaten you and crap like that.'

'What's happening?' said Angie. 'I can't see anyone in here. I don't know what's happening. What are you talking about?'

'I think I can hear water, Ang.' Kes held the light to her own face.

'Can't be water though, Kes. Even that mess of rocks we just came through was dry except for those two patches of mud.'

'Then the tunnel's acting like a pipe, trapping sound or something. It must be a chimney. A hole up to the outside. Maybe it's wind I can hear.'

'Get on with it, Kes,' said Jack. 'Get going, will you.'

The passage dropped sharply again. 'Am I imagining it,' Kes turned around to ask Angie, 'or it is getting lighter? Are my eyes playing tricks?'

'Don't know, Kes, all I can see is your back and the light of my torch.'

'It is,' Kes said, after another few paces. 'Look, you can make out some of that wall ahead. We're coming out into something,' she called back to the others. 'I think it's another entrance to the outside, I can hear the sound clearly now. It still sounds like wind — or water. But ... there can't be running water around here.'

'It'll be wind playing tunes around another entrance,' Finn said.

'… and I can see light. It's getting stronger all the time. Yes! Listen!' Kes shouted.

They could all see the faint light now, and hear the noise funnelling through the tunnel, which grew louder and louder with every turn.

'It isn't wind, it's water! I'm sure of it! But water? I can't believe it!' Kes shouted. 'There must be a whole river of water!'

They scrambled down the last steep curve, falling out of its end as the tunnel suddenly opened out again and dropped a metre into another cave. It was a long narrow winding cavern with a deep split in the roof running along its full length, flooding it with strange green daylight.

Water! A torrent of it roared out of a metre-wide hole to their right, at the near end of the cave wall, like a gigantic fire hydrant — a tumultuous, deafening cataract.

Kes flung up her hands in relief. It was great to be out of the tunnel and back in the light. They all felt it. The twins ran into the water, standing in the deluge, letting it push them around and pour over their bodies.

'Unreal! It's like being under the sea. I'm swimming,' shouted Jon, flapping his arms. 'This is wicked!'

'An underground river. The water's freezing,' Jack yelled.

'It's really strong. It'd knock you over if you stood in the middle,' Jon shouted over the roaring. 'It's awesome! This is what's carved out these caves and passages, isn't it, Kes? Over hundreds of years?'

Kes laughed. 'Try hundreds of thousands of years, at least.'

The green sunlight from the roof filtered down through a canopy of fernlike plants growing in the crack and hanging down into the cave high above their heads.

The waterspout, arching out of the wall, fell metres away into a series of pools carved out of the flat rock floor by an eternity of pounding water. The four pools poured into each other like a long string of beads and disappeared somewhere out of sight around a bend at the far end of the cave. The current running between the pools was strong enough to have carved out deep joining channels over the millennia.

'It's very beautiful, isn't it, Kes?' Sarah shouted, over the roar of the water.

'Yes — and it's better being out of those tunnels. That's what I like,' Kes shouted back. 'They weigh down on me. I feel like a blind mole in there.'

Jack, now lying on his belly, was gently stirring the sand in the bottom of the pool. 'There's not a trace of colour in here. Not a speck of gold,' he called disgustedly to Jon. 'There should be. These pools should be full of gold.'

'This is a fantastic cave.' Angie leapt across. 'This is my favourite. The one with the paintings is great, really interesting, but I love this one. Look at the plants up there, what on earth do they live on?'

'Sun, air, dissolved minerals out of the rock,' Kes said. 'Same as other plants. We just aren't used to looking at them from the roots up with a worm's-eye view.'

Jon was trying to figure out how he could join sticks together to reach up through the crack in the roof. The twins reckoned that if they tied a coloured rag onto the end they'd be able to find it from outside and come down on ropes through the fissure.

Finn had hardly spoken since they first entered the cave. He stood staring at the torrent of water pouring out of the wall. 'Do you think it's ours? The water, I mean. It's on our property, isn't it? Do we have water rights to it?'

Kes immediately caught his intent. 'Yes!' she shouted. 'It doesn't go anywhere, I mean, it doesn't come above ground anywhere on our place, does it? We've got to be able to use it. Jack, you're wrong! Completely wrong! These pools *are* full of gold!'

Angie grabbed her arm. 'Turn around. What are you saying? What about the water? What do you mean, "use it"?'

'Yes! Yes. Yes. Yes!!' Finn and Kes were jumping, punching the air.

'You mean we can pump it out, don't you? Use it on the paddocks?' The image of the ash bowls and blackened ground suddenly sprouting green sprang into Angie's mind.

'Geez! Will you look at it pouring out! Yeeehaaa!' Finn bellowed at the cave roof. 'We've found the biggest river this side of the Latrobe, and it's running under our place. It's fan-bloody-tastic!'

'We'll be able to water and restock even if the drought doesn't break for another year,' Sarah shouted. 'There's a sea of water pouring out of here, just running away underground.'

Jumping up and down, they screamed like maniacs, 'WE'VE FOUND WATER!!' 'WE'VE FOUND WATER!!'

'Now this!' Kes shrieked, jumping into a pool, '*This* is a gold strike. *This* is the luck of the Lawsons.'

'We've really found it! It's ours! Buckets of it — tonnes of it — a river of water! Can you believe it?' said Angie.

'We'll restock,' Finn said. 'We'll drop a pipe into the water through the crack up there. We could start pumping tomorrow, hook up the old water cannon, even if it's just the home paddock. I'd guess that's what we're under here. This water *is* liquid gold, just like they said to old Lawson last century. But it's more than that! We've saved the place, I swear it. We can stay!' he shouted at the roof. 'We can stay!'

He leapt into the pool with Kes as if he couldn't get enough of the water, flinging it at the others, laughing madly.

Angie, clutching Sarah, jumped up and down so hard she thought her teeth would break, saying over and over. 'We did it! We did it! We did it, Sarah! We can stay. Do you get it, Sarah? We're staying. You're not going anywhere. None of us are.'

'But where does it go?' Kes asked, climbing out after Finn and shaking the water off her shirt and shorts. 'Bloody hell, that water's cold! I swear it comes from under the roots of the Baw Baws.'

'Out this end somewhere. Come down here,' called Sarah, wading through the pools to the far end of the cave. 'It narrows into a sort of tail. The river runs out at the end. You can't see where it goes.'

They watched the water sliding smoothly away into a slot under the rock face at Sarah's feet.

'Where does it go?' asked Jon. 'It doesn't come to the surface.'

'Who knows?' Kes answered. 'Maybe this is what feeds the waterhole and stops it from ever drying up, even in this drought. Maybe it comes out at the spring in the bottom paddock when that runs. Perhaps that's why it dried up, usually more water runs though here. I don't know.'

Finn shook a spray of water from his hair. 'Maybe it doesn't ever come out, and it sinks down into the artesian basin. There obviously isn't a river running on the surface anywhere near here, just the dried-up creek in the home paddock, and that only runs in winter and spring.'

'Yeah,' said Kes. 'That's what confused me in the passage. I could hear a river running that couldn't exist.'

'So where are we now in relationship to the outside world?' Finn asked her. 'What are we under?'

'It must be on the far side of the valley wall,' Jack shouted. 'We've walked underground right through the ridge.'

'It was 918 steps, except for a few where the passage was broken up,' said Jon suddenly. 'I counted them from the painted cave. You're supposed to count your steps you know, for your map. Finn said so.'

'Good on you, Jon. You're the only one who remembered. You've got more brains than any of us,' said Kes. 'That's probably about four hundred metres from that cave, roughly; we've only been shuffling along in the tunnel. The painted cave's about the same distance — another four hundred metres — from the entrance, don't you think? That'd take us right through the hill, nearly a kilometre from the cave entrance. You might be right, Jack, if that's the direction we went in. I'm not a good rabbit; I get really confused when I can't see the sun. Should've brought a compass, I suppose they work underground. Do they, Finn?'

'I don't know. I suppose so — maybe. I'm having trouble working out where the cave system is lying under the gullies and ridges. I reckon the twins have the right idea. Poke something up through the crack that we can find from the outside.'

It was mid afternoon. They guessed that if they could manufacture something very long, like a series of sticks tied or nailed together, they'd be able to push a marker through the crack.

'That side of the ridge has been well and truly burnt,' Sarah said. 'You'd see a coloured rag from a hundred metres out there.'

There isn't one stick left on the whole place,' Jack said. 'But we could stay at the waterhole and cut some reeds,' Jon said. 'We've got enough string to tie them together and reach up through there.'

Kes wouldn't have a bar of it. 'Over my dead body. I don't trust you two as far as I can kick you. You're coming back to the house with me, or Finn's staying with you. Anyhow, I think reeds are too bend-able, we'll need to get some proper wood.'

They all wanted to go home that evening with a map of the water source, plonk it down on the dinner table and watch their parents' faces. Their fathers would be worn out; they were always dead-beat when they came in these days. Helen and Mai would be cranky after a day in Melbourne and the long drive back in the heat. But they were going to give them the best day they'd ever had! Kes wanted to be able to put her finger on a map of the property and say, 'Down this crack in the rock, right here, you can drop down a hose and pump out liquid gold. You said to find me a river, and we have.'

As they passed up the tunnel, through the rock falls and out into the painted cave, Kes felt a great weight tumbling from her. The families' troubles, their awful bleak future, had lifted and rolled away into a dark corner.

They wouldn't have to leave the Baw Baws. Her heart leapt. The water assured her of that. She knew that if she didn't have to leave she'd somehow work out who she was and what she was all about, lose this horrible feeling that she'd been split down the middle and was arguing with herself.

Kes took a last look at the spirit man and whispered, 'Thank you, whatever your name is, whatever you are.'

Did he blink at her or was it the flickering light of her torch?

They could see their fathers' truck and Mai's car as they approached the house.

'They're all home! Fantastic!' Kes shouted out the cab window to the others in the back.

Pat and Charlie had come back to repair the handle of the wire strainer which was broken in two. Mai, Kate, and Brian had just arrived back from Melbourne. Their mothers were frazzled and Brian looked miserable. The six kids leapt out of the ute, all shouting at once.

Their parents were standing around the remains of the burnt-out cattle race. Charlie, welding rod in his hand, was working on the broken handle and listening angrily to Mai relaying the advice from the Melbourne solicitors. It was not good news. Pat looked desperate, and Kate kicked at a fence post, her mind rapidly juggling figures.

Kes flung herself into her father's arms. 'We've found you a river!' she sobbed.

Pat held her at arm's length and searched her face, sudden worry flashing into his eyes.

Kate swung around. 'What are you talking about?'

'We found a river. Deep in a cave. Down near the waterhole.'

'There's no such thing. There aren't any caves here.'

'There is. We found it. Emma found it,' said Sarah. 'It's really big, the passages go on forever and there's a cave painted with Aboriginal hands and a spirit person and a cave where a river comes out of a wall like a great fire hydrant, and other ones too.'

'True, Mum,' Kes said. 'Down at the end there's a cave with an underground river in it.'

'What cave? There isn't a cave within fifty ks of here.'

'There is, Mum, we found it last week.'

'There can't be.' Kate looked around at Finn. He was shouting the same things at Mai and Charlie. They were arguing as well.

'It's true, Dad,' Finn shook his father, 'don't keep saying, "There isn't a river … there isn't a cave", like a bloody broken record. I tell you there is, we've just come out of it. Look at us. We're still wet.'

'You can't be. There can't be a river. There can't be a cave.'

'Dad! You're driving me nuts! Listen to me. We have found a river. Underground in a cave. Near the waterhole.'

'An underground cave? By the waterhole?'

'Stop repeating everything and believe me! We have found water!'

Mai and Charlie looked around at Pat and Kate. Kate shook her head at them. 'I don't know what they're talking about either. OK. Come here the lot of you and explain this to us again. Simply.'

'All right. From the start.'

Finn started and stopped, then laughed and pointed at Brian. 'It's all his doing really. Brian started all this!' He raised Brian's arm in a triumphant salute.

'Yes!' shouted Kes. 'Brian got lost and found the emu egg that became Emma. Emma discovered the cave ...'

'Only because we took Ang and Sarah up there looking for gold,' said Jon.

'Only because the gully was burnt out. You couldn't get through before that,' said Jack, 'and we found this cave and these passages and other caves that led in from the entrance ...'

'Excuse *me*, Jack! *We* did. Emma, Sarah and I

found the cave, then we showed you,' Angie said indignantly. 'You were off grubbing around in the dirt as usual.'

Kes interrupted, 'We only went into the caves we knew were safe.'

'Because Kes got scared. So did Sarah.'

'Shut up, Jack.' Sarah kicked him. 'You're an idiot. You'd have lost us, the way you wanted to hoon around in there like a moron.'

'Caves? What? Is there more than one?'

'It's a whole system. We think it goes on forever,' Angie said. 'There are tunnels that join caves and other ones that we've no idea where they go.'

'We found a cave painted with handprints and a spirit person, with stalactites on the roof.' Kes searched the adults' faces, but found only stunned disbelief. 'Then there's a part where there's been a massive rock fall. Then more tunnel, then a water cave, where the water pours out of the wall. It's got a great split in the roof. We came back to get wood to nail together and make a pole long enough to reach up through that crack. We figured we'd be able to find a flag from the outside.'

'We think we must be under the back of the home paddock, Dad,' Finn said, 'probably in among those rough gullies that the cattle stay out of. You know, where the rock strata are all on edge, and it's — it was — a tangle of undergrowth before the fire. You couldn't force your way through there. I know I've never explored all of it. Probably no one ever has, except the Kurnai.'

'But that's all we need!' shouted Pat. 'All we need is the one lucky break. Enough water to carry us over to the rains.'

'Are you sure?' Kate asked, 'You haven't all gone suddenly mad, have you?'

'Mum! Look at me. Watch my lips. We have found a river,' Kes said slowly. 'It is huge. It is underground. It is in a cave. We have all seen it, and all been in it. It has real, wet water in it. Is this true, Finn, or is this not?'

Finn nodded.

'It's old Lawson's river of gold!' Charlie shouted. 'It's Lawsons' luck. Come on! What are you all standing here for? Show me. Take us to it. Hop in the trucks. I won't believe you've found any river until I'm wet as well ... You are sure, aren't you, Finn?'

'Dad! Get in the truck, will you?'

An hour and a half later, all eleven of them, including Brian, were soaked through and splashing around in the pools in the water cave. Pat and Charlie, so excited that they hardly knew what to do with themselves, were fighting under the water pouring out of the wall.

Finn and Kes laughed at them — they were behaving like the twins. Still, it was good to hear

Charlie yell, when he'd broken free of Pat's headlock, 'You know what this means, don't you?'

They nodded, hours ahead of him in that line of thinking. 'We can pump mega-litres out of here. Green up the home paddock at least, in this heat it'll grow like crazy. Get that old water cannon running again. Won't know what's hit it after a two year holiday.'

'When the grass will support it, we'll restock it with those few breeders that survived up in the gully over the back of Black Jack Spur,' said Pat.

'The bank'll listen now. We'll eventually cut down the debt to an amount that we can handle again.' Kate laughed with relief.

'We can stay here!' Charlie punched the air and pushed Pat into the pool again. 'You little rippers.' He shook Brian by the hand. 'Good man, Brian. Could've killed you when you pinched that emu egg … but it's turned out all right, eh? Good man! Yes, we can stay! Oh yes! We can stay all right!'

'I was never leaving, anyhow,' Sarah said to Angie.

As the two families climbed out of the gully, Kes stopped on the high ridge that looked over towards the houses and beyond them, down the valley into Federation. In the far distance a kestrel hunted, its cry drifting across the hills.

She watched the others below her, following the

rough roo track down the hill to the waterhole, and shook herself like old Blue. Suddenly all her self-doubt didn't seem to matter any more. It didn't even seem real. These were the things that were real to her, spread out in front of her. These people, her family, her land, this sky with not a cloud in it. The waterhole with the grinding hollow and the cockies' tree. The houses on the hill, stark against the grey ash, old Freda, forlorn under the skeletal remains of a burnt-out pepper tree. These were the things that were precious, and no matter how bad it all looked to anyone else, it was their land and they were staying on it.

She laughed. For the first time in months, she felt confident. Energetic, alive again. Everything would sort out, the water would start to flow and the paddocks would spring up fast in the heat. They'd all go out and round up the remaining cattle from behind Black Jack Spur. Gill would come home, school would start again and everything would settle back to normal.

Looking down on the waterhole, their clothes lying so casually on the sand, a currawong perched on the rim of the lunch basket, another on a tent rope, the ute sitting there with one door open and their equipment still in the back, it felt like an ordinary summer day, and they were heading down to the waterhole for a picnic.

In the lead, Sarah held Angie's hand and was arguing with Jack. Finn and Brian, above them, were walking along the high ridge, Finn pointing to something down by the waterhole. Sarah looked up at them, laughing, then turned and called back something to Jon that Kes didn't catch. Emma, happy to have found Angie again, was flapping up and down the hillside around her.

Kes's heart turned over with love for them. That such a serious threat of separation could have come to them was beyond contemplation.

Charlie and Pat were surveying the paddocks from the vantage point of the ridge. Finn and Brian caught up to them and Charlie put his arm around Finn. Pat was explaining something to Brian. Kes guessed from the hand waving that they were deciding where to start the refencing of the home paddock. That was a high priority now.

Kes felt a core of happiness settle within her that she knew could not be extinguished. She looked across the paddocks to the mountains. In a couple of years this would all be green again, her beautiful, smiling, blue and green land.

Chapter 19

IT WAS DURING dinner that night that Kes announced she had something to tell them.

'Oh good, more surprises! What is it this time?' asked Kate, 'Emeralds, silver, diamonds? We've had some gold. You didn't find more while you were ferreting around in the caves, did you? You had plenty of time! But something else different, please, to break the monotony of this boring gold and water!'

'Well — I've got a gem, but it's more like a — like a black opal.'

She pulled a letter out of her pocket. 'I got this yesterday, but things have been a bit hectic between then and now. I hope you think this is all right, Dad.' She looked at him, suddenly anxious, 'I hope you're pleased. I hoped you would be, but now it's here, I feel ... I don't know ...' She stopped short.

The table was suddenly silent. No one in the room, except Finn, had a clue what she was talking about. She shot him a look.

He grinned at her and stuck his thumbs up. 'Go, Kes! You can do it.'

'Just get on with it, kiddo,' said Pat, smiling. 'Nothing can shock me any more. Unless you tell me the river's a myth and the water only in my wild imagination.'

'All right, but sometimes ... most of the time, I wasn't sure if I was doing the right thing or not. You have to understand. Do you understand?'

'No,' said Pat, bemused, 'I understand nothing. If I've no idea what you're talking about, how can I possibly? You're going in circles, Kes. Say what you have to say, then I'll tell you.'

'Well, I thought I could ... but then ... Some of the people were so awful ... that horrible, lying Hatty woman, for instance, she told me it was none of my business, but it is really. I think so anyway.' She stopped again.

Pat laughed at her. 'For crying out loud! Just spit it out, Kes, then we'll all know what you're dithering about.'

'Well — oh hell, I'll just read it. It's from Murringundi in New South Wales. Up on the Queensland border.'

'Dear Kes and Pat,' Kes read, glancing at her father.

'I can hardly write this without crying. When I heard from Rose Bannock that you were still alive, Pat, I couldn't believe it.

'We all thought you'd gone forever. We, that is, me, Margaret, and one of your brothers, Paul, who lives in Victoria; we've been trying to find you for years.'

She heard her father gasp and plunged ahead, not daring to look at him.

'I'm afraid we thought you might have died because we could never find any trace of you beyond that awful farm you ran away from years ago, when you were just a kid.'

The people around the table were absolutely still.

'My God,' breathed Pat. 'You've found my family, haven't you?'

Kes nodded. There was a huge lump in her throat.

Kate jumped up and flung her arms around Pat, who looked as if he was going to howl. Her eyes were shining with tears. 'Go on, Kes,' she urged.

'I want you to know that our mum is still alive, although she is now over seventy and getting frail. There's nothing wrong with her spirit though — she can't wait to see you.

'I don't know how much you know about us. From what Kes told Rose, you can't remember very much, but you were only two when you were taken.

'You have Mum, Grace Chalmers, and her sister Iris; then there's me — I'm your sister Margaret Tyne, and your twin brothers, Paul and Matthew Chalmers. Paul and his wife Janey live in Victoria, in a town called Moe. Do you know it? Rose said it was close.'

Pat laughed, but only in place of tears. 'Paul

Chalmers, that cheeky little bugger I used to play footy against — my brother! Jesus Christ, the last time I played against him, I flattened him! Thought I'd knocked him out. I got two weeks for that. Well, I'll be damned. Paul Chalmers! I suppose I could do worse than him in a lucky dip.'

'I hate those bloody Chalmers kids,' Jon grumbled. 'Now they're our cousins. Geez!'

'You'd reckon she could've found out first,' Jack muttered. 'Once you've got 'em you can't dump 'em.'

'Matthew and his wife Clare still live near us here. Matt's a mechanic in Murringundi, when he's not working with us. We have a cattle station in the middle of nowhere. If you stick your finger in the middle of the NSW and Queensland border, you're close.

'We've got twelve kids between us all, so Kes, Sarah and the twins suddenly have a dozen more cousins! And that's just your closest relatives. There are lots of old people here in our mob who still remember you, Pat.

'Mum says she won't sleep properly again until she sees you all. I know this'll be a big shock to you finding out you've got a family, but we do want to see you as soon as we can.

'Your loving sister, Margaret.

'PS. I still can't believe it, Pat. It's my birthday and Kes has given me the best birthday present I've ever had.'

Kes stopped reading. Pat stood up, walked around the table, and folded her up in his arms. He stood rocking her gently, while his tears dripped down onto her head.

Chapter 20

SEVERAL DAYS BEFORE Brian was due to return home, Finn and Angie had to spend the day in Morwell with Mai. They both needed dental checks and new shoes, and Finn had grown so rapidly over the holidays that he had no clothes which still fitted him except one pair of shorts. Sarah went to keep Angie company.

Kes and Brian took the twins to the waterhole. Kes sneaked a look at Brian sitting beside her in the cab of the ute in Finn's usual seat. He was smiling, watching the water cannon arcing water across the home paddock. Five very skittish young calves leapt and ran every time it pulsed in their direction. They were the start of a new generation of cattle. They ran on a sparse cover of green and their hoofs kicked up no dust.

'You even look different,' Kes said impulsively.

Brian laughed, 'It's that dirty waterhole that did it. Something in the water, wasn't it?'

'Oh, please! Don't remind me!' Kes sneaked another look at him, 'No, you do. You're browner and skinnier to start with. You've changed a lot. Three and a half weeks … It seems longer, doesn't it?'

'It's like a year.' He was silent for a long time and then said, 'I decided I was going to talk to Mum, stop trying to avoid it. Part of my new "truth at all costs and no bullshit" policy, I suppose. I wanted to do it before I went home, before Dad came out of hospital. I talked to her last night.'

Kes had wondered if he'd tell them about the call. She watched the track, dodging potholes, waiting for him to continue.

'How is she? Is she feeling any better?' Kes tried to sound encouraging, to disguise the fact that she couldn't care less how Brian's mother felt, except that it affected her son.

'It's a lifetime ago since you first brought me down here on the back of your old red truck, isn't it? What a horrible weekend. I was so angry that day I thought I could self-combust.' He rubbed his face. 'It's like remembering a different person, Kes … I think … I hope, that is, I'm a different person. I hope like hell I've changed … but how can I — or anyone — change so much so quickly? I must be pretty sketchy, eh? Or it's not real, just another famous pretence in the life of Brian.'

Kes shook her head. 'No. It was hard for you that first time you were here. You didn't know any of us except Angie and, as I clearly remember, she was the only one who was friendly to you.'

Brian's face softened, 'Angie's my mate. She says I was good to her in hospital, but I think the nurses used to let me talk to her so I'd stay sane. She did me more good than I ever did her.' He gave Kes a funny look, 'It wasn't only that weekend though, that's how I was all the time, at home and at school. I don't ever want to go back to being that angry. One minute you're furious, the next you feel like a real jerk. I'll never forget the way you all looked at me that weekend, especially you and Finn, as if I should've been kept in a jar.'

'No. It was …'

'How can I stop myself changing back again? How can I make these new ideas stick? I could just slide back into the same bad habits.'

'It's not stuck on the outside of you, you idiot. It's not going to wash off in the waterhole, you know.'

'Isn't it? How do you know?'

'Because … because … Well, for a start, because you can see something you want to change. That's a huge thing to do. You won't go back to what you've been unless you want to, and then you'll know what you're doing. And for another thing, you won't be able to kid yourself any more. You won't ever believe your own bullshit again.'

Brian watched a heron lift off from the edge of the swamp, turn and flap slowly overhead. 'It eats you up behaving like that, pretending you're so smart, knowing every one thinks you're a freak and won't have anything to do with you. The kids I like most at school think I'm weird. It's really only my friend Andrew who puts up with me, and that's probably because he's in the same boat, so he has to. His father's on an assault charge for hitting his mother and then getting stuck into the police. Andrew's mother took out a restraining order on him. He's not allowed anywhere near their house. I suppose we don't have to pretend much around each other. Everyone else gives us a wide berth.'

'Maybe people don't basically change,' Kes said slowly, trying to form the thoughts as she spoke. 'Perhaps your soul or your brain, or whatever drives you, just waits for the chance to break out and become the real person it couldn't be before. Maybe it could take years, until you've left home even. Parts of you might stay hidden for years, unless they're jumped on and forced out into the open. It's like jumping on something squashy. You change under pressure. The bigger the jumps and thumps, the more you change. So, how comfortable does that make you feel?'

'Like I should be covered in green ectoplasmic slime with the old me shrouded underneath, just a finger or two showing out of the ooze.' Brian laughed. 'You're such a bucket full of surprises, Kes!'

'So are you!'

'I feel ... good, I think. But I'm worried that things'll wear me down when I go home. I'll lose my new slimy coat.'

'Things'll be very different with your mother away. Maybe it'll be easier with just the two of you for the next month.'

'I'll feel a lot more secure when I've had more practice at this new "no bullshit, no lies" plan. When you're used to living like that, telling them is second nature. You don't know why you do it, and after a while you don't even think about it. You say the first thing that comes into your head. It's easier.' He paused, 'This is so embarrassing. What a jerk. No wonder I don't want to think of myself as the same person.'

'Do you think it'll be harder when you go home? Is that what worries you? Do you think things'll be worse between your parents?'

Brian drew a deep breath. 'When I spoke to Mum, she said she wasn't coming back home. She's left Dad and me. She's going to live with Johnnie when she gets out of hospital. She said she "preferred to stay with Johnnie because he respects her." Brian snorted. 'Johnnie Pike's never respected anything in his life except money and flashy cars. Mum says Johnnie's fun and she loves him "and he doesn't have a bad heart." She said she "wasn't cut out to be a nursemaid." I didn't think, even after all this, she could be so ... mercenary.'

Brian stared out the window, his face pale under his suntan. Kes could see tears glistening in his eyes. She leaned over and took his hand briefly.

'Would you come back and spend the next school holidays with us?' she asked.

'Don't you think I might've worn everyone's patience a bit thin after all this mess?'

'No. Idiot.'

'Do you think Finn'd agree with you?'

'Of course. I'm certain of it.'

'Do you want me to?'

'Didn't I just ask you?'

'OK then.' Brian leaned across and kissed her cheek. Kes was so surprised she drove into a pothole. Her cheek burnt like fire.

Chapter 21

O N THE DAY that her grandmother came, Kes was working with her father in the home paddock.

Brian had returned home the day before. His father had been discharged from the rehabilitation hospital and his mother hadn't changed her decision to leave them. She'd already told Brian's father. She tried to speak to Brian again but he was still too angry with her. She said she'd try again when he came to his senses, then sent him a soppy card with a hundred-dollar bill in it. Brian tried to give it to Mai to pay for his food, but she refused to take it, and Finn saw him give it away to an old man on the street in Federation.

Kes and Pat were manhandling the heavy hose that snaked out of the cleft in the cave roof. Their biggest pump sucked water from the river rushing beneath their feet and shot it out through the water cannon. Water arced in immense spraying plumes, around and around, creeping across the paddocks, working miracles on the burnt earth and leaving, after only days, a fragile carpet of green in its wake.

About nine-thirty Pat paused, laid down the

section of hose they were untangling along the track, and said quietly to Kes, 'My mother — your grand-mother — is coming.'

Kes stared at him. 'What! When? Why didn't you tell us?'

'I didn't know. I know now.'

Kes was dumbfounded. 'How do you know?'

'I just do. She's quite near.' Without another word he put down his tools and started across the pad-docks towards the gate.

Kes watched his stride grow longer and faster, until he was running. Running to intercept the car that was appearing out of the eucalypts along the house track.

Through a gap in the trees, she saw him spring out onto the track and the car slow to a halt. She saw a tiny frail old woman open the passenger door and walk the short distance that divided them. She came to a halt in front of her son. She saw her take his arm, turn it and search for the birthmark on the back of his elbow.

Although only a few words and several shy glances passed between them, they contained two life-times of infinite sadness and joy.

The old woman put her hand on her son's arm and they turned towards where Kes stood. She started down the track to them.

Behind the figures of her father and grand-mother, the house track suddenly seemed to roll out and reach on forever, across the mountain range, over rivers and creeks to the great inland plains of the Queensland border. Kes was conscious of the hidden river running beneath her feet. She had the vision of her river and her narrow road connected into a vast network of other roads and other rivers, along which, over a lifetime, this old woman and this man, her father, had been moving, to link together at last in this place. At this moment, on this track, their ways had finally met, the intricate patterns of two lives unfolding behind them. An immense circle of thousands of kilometres, enclosing four decades of lives, was finally reaching its completion.

Kes pulled up sharply in front of her grandmother. Despite the surge of happiness that rushed through her, she felt incredibly shy. She gazed at her feet, finding it hard to lift her head.

Her grandmother reached up to touch her face.

'Hello, Kes,' she said. 'You've done very well to do this thing. It's been a long time, this thirty-eight years.'

Behind her, Kes could hear the pounding of Sarah's feet as she came flying down the track, and the shouts of the twins following. She glanced at her father and saw the familiar brown eyes smiling back at her, the same eyes that she found in her grandmother's etched face, even the same three worry lines between their eyebrows. She took her grandmother's eloquent hands.

She turned to watch her family. They were all

coming now. Everyone from both families. Kes watched with infinite happiness, the months of self-doubt evaporating.

Behind her, other people were getting out of the car. Relatives she knew only on paper. A great aunt as old as her grandmother, a cousin her own age and her aunt Margaret, she guessed.

She laughed out loud. Here on this hot summer day, still in the middle of an unrelenting drought, in the middle of a burnt-out world, she couldn't imagine greater happiness than this circle of her family closing around her.